WAIT FOR THE JUDGE

In that part of Nevada, cattlemen and farmers were poised on the brink of disaster. Would a farmer's son live to be tried for the killing of a cattleman, or would vengeance-crazed cowhands overrun the county jail and take the law into their own hands? Between the warring factions stood two trouble-shooting Texans, both doggedly opposed to lynch law and ready to demonstrate their opposition with rock-hard fists and blazing six-guns.

WAIT FOR THE JUDGE

In that part of Nevada, cattlemen and farmers were poised on the brink of disaster. Would a farmer's son live to be tried for the killing of a cattleman, or would vengeance-crazed cowhands overrun the county jail and take the law into their own hands? Between the warring factions stood two trouble-shooting Texans, both doggedly opposed to lynch law and ready to demonstrate their opposition with rock-hard fists and blazing six-guns.

MARSHALL GROVER

WAIT FOR THE JUDGE

A Larry & Stretch Western

Complete and Unabridged

First published in Australia in 1980 by
Horwitz Grahame Pty Limited
Australia

First Linford Edition
published September 1995
by arrangement with
Horwitz Grahame Pty Limited
Australia

British Library CIP Data

Grover, Marshall
    Larry & Stretch: Wait for the judge.
    —Large print ed.—
    Linford western library
    I. Title II. Series
    823 [F]

    ISBN 0–7089–7758–8

Published by
F. A. Thorpe (Publishing) Ltd.
Anstey, Leicestershire

Set by Words & Graphics Ltd.
Anstey, Leicestershire
Printed and bound in Great Britain by
T. J. Press (Padstow) Ltd., Padstow, Cornwall

This book is printed on acid-free paper

1

Going it Alone

THEIR chosen campsite appeared tranquil at this hour, 8 a.m. of a clear spring morning, but their conversation contrasted sharply with their surroundings. The much-traveled Texas Trouble-Shooters had found their way to the Gillette Hills of West Nevada an ideal base for a few weeks of hunting and fishing and living the lazy life, a bend of a cheerfully-chattering stream.

They had been together a long time, these compulsive nomads from the Lone Star State, so maybe they were entitled to wrangle once in a while. Right now, for a wonder, it was the usually-placid Stretch Emerson who wrangled, cussed and ranted, while Larry Valentine squatted beside his stashed gear and surveyed him boredly.

"Ain't the first time you've said it!" raged the taller Texan. A shaggy-maned, homely beanpole, he towered a full 3 inches over the 6 feet 3 inches tall Larry. And now he trudged back and forth in his trail-dusty range clothes, angrily brandishing his fists. "What am I — useless or somethin'? You think I can't ride from here to Cleaver . . . ?"

"Keever," corrected Larry. "That trapper we met up with yesterday, he called it Keever. Seat of Keever County — about three and a half miles straight east of these hills."

"So it's Keever and it's real close and we need supplies, and you're gripin' about how you can't send me into any town by myself!" accused Stretch. "A little chore like that — I can't handle by myself?"

"Any other time," Larry said mildly, "same damn thing always happened, didn't it? Without me along to side you, somethin' crazy always happens

2

to you. There's trouble. You end up in the local calaboose and I got to go talk you out of whatever fix you got yourself into."

"That's an insult!" gasped Stretch. "You're sayin' it again! Consarn you, runt, I got feelin's just like any other hombre — got pride too . . . !"

"And I'm hurtin' your pride," jibed Larry. "Well, pardon me all to hell."

He rose and, arms akimbo, traded hard stares with the gangling hellion who had sided him through better than 20 years of hectic, nerve-wracking knight-errantry. Yes, it had to be more than 20 years, because they were only in their mid-teens, tall for their age and runaways from a Texas cowtown schoolhouse, when they enlisted in the Confederate Cavalry. Brawny, dark-haired and ruggedly handsome, he too wore range clothes topped off by the inevitable sweat-stained Stetson, but only half as much Colt as his partner. Unlike Stretch, he was not ambidexterous with handguns. He was the thinking half of this trouble-prone duo and still husky. Physically anyway. Mentally, he was prematurely aged, more than a little cynical. Trouble-shooting, so many years of it, had soured him somewhat, and maybe he was insensitive to Stretch's feelings, maybe too much inclined to take him for granted.

"We got scarce any coffee or tobacco and no booze," he pointed out. "No canned grub. Scarce anything to eat. So, if I let you ride to Keever alone, you'd better be back by mid-afternoon with everything we need. You leave me here hungry and cravin' a smoke, I'm gonna get real mean."

"You're *always* real mean!" retorted Stretch. "Always sarcastical too! Always talkin' down to me like I'm some clumsy lamebrain! If you *let* me ride in alone you say? The hell with it! I'm goin' anyway, like it or not! Since when've I gotta have your doggone permission to ride three and a half miles to buy supplies?"

Larry grimaced irritably and produced the wallet containing their combined bankroll. Cash? Of recent times, they'd had plenty. Thanks to their luck at poker, dice and roulette, they were solvent to the tune of $1000.00, give or take a dollar or two. Peeling a couple of bills from the roll, Larry offered them. Stretch snatched and pocketed the money, still glowering at him.

"I should write you a list?" asked Larry.

"That's *another* insult!" yelled the taller Texan; it was getting to where Larry could not say the right thing. "As if I dunno what we need! Flour and salt and canned grub, coffee, tobacco, a couple quarts of rye whiskey, matches, bread, some steaks, sowbelly and beans, dried apples . . . "

"So you know what we want — fine," shrugged Larry. "Go fetch it. And don't hustle on my account. If you're all that sure you can stay out of trouble, hang around, see the sights, socialize with the citizens, say howdy to the sheriff."

"Wouldn't think of leavin' you to starve," Stretch said caustically, as he moved to his horse. "I'll likely be back by noon."

He made short work of readying his mount for the trail. Nothing more was said, but Larry was more amused than impressed by his partner's resentful silence. He prepared for the short wait while, at a steady clip, Stretch rode his clean-limbed pinto eastward through the hills. They had been together a long time, Larry reflected. Too much of their own company, too much to expect harmony every hour of every day of the rough years since Appomattox.

Rough was putting it mild. They had been hounded by their hex ever since quitting the Lone Star State, surrendering to their wanderlust and mutually agreeing they should see a little of the country before returning to settle in their home-state. So much for good intentions. They had seen a great deal of the frontier, had been as far north as the Canadian border and, on more than one occasion, quite some distance into Mexico. They had seen San Francisco and the blue Pacific and they were still wandering, suffering a permanent case of itchy feet. Settle down? No chance. Always another mountain to be climbed, another river to be crossed.

Frontier journalists had described them as trouble-prone, and with some justification. Try as they might, they could not dodge their destiny. It seemed fate had decreed they should stumble into violent conflict wherever they showed their sun-browned noses. Peace-loving they claimed to be, also law-abiding, but the same could not be said for the scores of desperadoes, stage robbers, bank bandits and rustlers, rogues of every variety, with whom they had locked horns. With the ordinary folk they could get along; each of them was gregarious in his own way. But the lawless were their sworn enemies and they had learned to defend themselves. Their survival instincts were strong, their hard-muscled bodies criss-crossed with old scars, legacies of life or death battles against the homicidal scum of the outlaw trails.

Keever proved to be a sizeable township and a replica of a hundred and one cattle, farming or mining centres the Texans had seen in their wandering years. Same plank sidewalks, false-fronted buildings lining a broad and dusty main street, narrower streets angling off to north and south of it. What could be said of Keever that could not be said for all the other towns? There were more saloons than churches, as usual, and there were the other standard edifices such as the town hall, the courthouse, the Western Union office and stage depot, plus the stores, livery stables and the expected three varieties of accommodation — impressive hotels for the well-heeled, not so impressive hotels for the ordinary transient and cheap doss-houses for the lowly.

Keever had something else, something

all too familiar to Woodville Eustace Emerson. He was conscious of it a few moments after entering Main Street. An atmosphere. A certain tension in the air. People on the sidewalks paid little attention to the new arrival. No old timers called a howdy or aimed a welcoming nod in his direction. As he rode past, it seemed all eyes were on the East End area, and he was at first tempted to wheel his mount and travel backward or swing into a side street.

"Whatever's happenin', pay no mind," he chided himself. "Whatever it is, it ain't none of your business anyway."

There was, in that part of Main Street fronting the sheriff's office and county jail, a heavy concentration of ranch-hands. Could this be pay-day for the Keever County spreads? Hell, no. This was Tuesday. So why weren't those waddies on home range, hunting strays or branding new calves or just flopping around the bunkhouse? Having asked himself this question, he gave himself the same answer. None of his business.

Well to the fore, his voice raised, was a lean young cowhand whose pearl-butted Colt was tied low at his right leg, a show-off whose sombrero was worn aslant on his dark head. He was calling jeering remarks to whoever listened to him from inside the law office. Stretch closed his ears to the taunting challenge and veered toward the nearest general store, dismounted at the hitchrail and, having looped his rein, moved inside to make his purchases.

The skinny fellow behind the counter refrained from offering an explanation for the prevailing tension and Stretch refrained from asking questions. He listed his needs, paid for them and saw them packed into a gunny sack. The skinny man secured the neck with a length of twine. Stretch thanked him, pocketed his change and trudged out to tie the sack to his saddle. And then, try as he might, he could no longer ignore what was happening in front of the law office.

"Come out and talk to us — if you

can work up the nerve, Pooley!" yelled the lean waddy with the low-slung pistol.

"That's tellin' him, Johnny," chuckled one of his buddies. "Now he's just *gotta* come out — that fool badge-toter — or admit he's yellow."

The sheriff emerged from the office, crossed his porch and descended the steps. He was 40 or thereabouts, paunchy and obviously apprehensive. Stretch got that impression while giving him credit for trying to talk turkey to these hotheads.

"Now, boys . . . " Pooley grinned appealingly. "Let's have no more of this hollerin' and cussin', huh? Ride on home and . . . "

"You know what we're here for, Pooley!" growled the man with the low-slung pistol. "Now quit stallin' and go fetch that stinkin' sodbuster! If you think Diamond Seven's gonna wait for some lawyer to smart-talk a jury . . . !"

"Hold on now, Johnny Button,"

protested the lawman. "Young Ezra's got his rights just like any other man. He's bein' held for trial and that trial will start just as soon as Judge Mayo gets here. Ain't long to wait. Why, it's less'n a couple weeks."

"The sodbuster killed Dacey Hargrove!" snarled Button.

"Maybe the judge'll call it manslaughter," countered Pooley. "It ain't for you to say — you or me. Up to the judge. You got to remember Dacey and young Ezra was in a fight. Couple bucks get to tradin' blows, one of 'em has to be hurt. It's too bad Dacey got killed, but I don't know if we can call it murder."

"*I* call it murder — so you're callin' me a liar!" accused Button. He was quick to seize this opportunity. "Pooley, I'm demandin' satisfaction!"

The bullying tactics continued while, covertly, Stretch studied the reaction of the trio on the sidewalk directly opposite the store, three elderly locals in town suits, one obviously a clergyman,

12

the other two derby-hatted, prosperous looking, typical civic leaders. They were trading comments and following the action anxiously, but making no move to intervene, at least not yet.

Pooley was sweating now in an agony of apprehension, sidling toward the trio, striving to placate his challenger.

"Stand your ground and fight!" ordered Button. "C'mon, Pooley! Prove you're worthy of that tin star — if you got the guts! Make your play!"

"I — I ain't drawin' against you, Johnny Button," mumbled Pooley. He was pallid and trembling, fumbling to unstrap his gunbelt. "The hell with it! They don't pay me enough to — get shot at by gunslick herders!" He let his sidearm drop to the dust while the Diamond Seven hands guffawed derisively. Whirling, he tugged off his badge and flung it toward the three civic leaders. "I quit, damn it! I'm gettin' out of Keever while I still got my health!"

"Pooley, you can't run now!" gasped

13

the shortest of the three. "The deputies have been scared off. That leaves only you and Cobb — and him drunk most of the time. If *you* go . . . "

"Ain't no 'if' about it," groaned Pooley. "I'm tellin' you, Mayor Keele, you couldn't pay me enought to make me stay."

"Don't you realize these hooligans mean to lynch young Gregg?" challenged the austere gent with the gold watch-chain. "Confound it, Pooley, a lynching would set this town back twenty years. There'd be no respect for law and order . . . "

"Don't make me no speeches, Mister Quinn." Pooley shook his head vehemently. "You're a banker. What would *you* know about — about how it feels to have a bullet plow through you? It happened to me at Gettysburg and, damn it, it ain't gonna happen again. And you, Reverend Wallace . . . " He pointed to the portly, black-garbed parson. "Don't try preachin' at me. The Lord helps him that helps himself — remember? So I'm helpin' myself right out of Keever!"

With that, the ex-sheriff of Keever County took to his heels. He was almost run down by four more cowhands riding fast along Main to join the bunch in front of the jail. They reined up in a flurry of dust, one of them brandishing a rope and yelling to Button.

"What the hell're we waitin' for?"

"Ain't waitin' no more, boys," grinned Button. "We got rid of Pooley, so all we got to do is go on in and drag Gregg out."

"Where we gonna hang him, Johnny?" demanded the man with the rope. "Hey! How about right here in the street?"

"How about a tree in Council Valley?" chuckled Button. "For his old man and all his sodbuster pals to see?"

Stretch was temporarily hypnotized. The girl who had dashed along the sidewalk to position herself below the law office steps, to spread her arms and

15

plead with the men surging toward her, was young, slender, garbed in checked gingham and so pretty, at least to Stretch, that his throat became dry. The eyes were big and brown and expressive and, as she raised her voice to make herself heard, his heart went out to her. He was smitten. For her, he was ready to fight all of these rioters — and there were at least two dozen of them.

"My brother's entitled to a fair trail! You can't do this! Oh, Lord, he didn't mean to kill your friend — didn't even start that fight!"

"Somebody hustle her out of here," ordered Button. "Her whinin' plagues my nerves. Go on. *Move* her!"

It spoke volumes for the hostility between cattle-men and farmers in this territory, the way three of Button's pals hurried to obey his command. Chivalry was dead in Keever until Stretch reacted. In a matter of moments, he had crossed the street and was joining the quartet by the porch steps, the

16

girl recoiling, struggling to break free of the man grasping her arm, one of his companions reaching for the other arm, the third man growling a warning to the tall stranger.

"Butt out, saddlebum!"

Thomas Joseph Quinn, owner and manager of the Quinn Trust Bank, nudged the mayor and said tensely, "It's getting worse, Bill. The stranger can expect no mercy from those rowdies."

"Our sheriff on the run and only a rumpot jailer between young Gregg and a lynch-party," muttered Billy Keele. "Well, Reverend, you got anything to say?"

"I'm praying for a miracle," frowned Parson Wallace.

Later, the civic leaders would remember Wallace's words and wonder if the stranger's intervention were the answer to his prayer or just coincidence. The girl's arm was free now, her assailant loosing a startled yell; Stretch had discouraged him by seizing an

17

ear and twisting. The second man promptly swung a punch to Stretch's face. Stretch grimaced, grasped that one by his collar, got his other hand to the collar of the waddy with the aching ear and batted their heads together with such ferocity that they flopped to their knees, dazed. The third man lashed out savagely. Stretch blocked the blow and retaliated with a roundhouse right that sent him spinning into the street to collide with the grim-faced Johnny Button. He then politely requested the wide-eyed girl to move up to the porch and began a vain attempt to reason with the hellion with the low-slung Colt.

"Now listen, kid, you ought to know better'n to faze a sheriff and make lynch-talk. 'Fore anybody else gets hurt, why don't you give up on it — and take your proddy friends away from here?"

Button was suddenly florid.

"How d'you like the nerve of this no-account?" he raged. "Who the hell does he think he is?"

"Nobody special," shrugged Stretch.

"Just a stranger passin' through." He jerked a thumb. "Let's have no more trouble, huh? Just vamoose — peaceable."

"That does it!" breathed Button. He retreated a few yards to stand poised for action, right hand hovering over his low-slung gunbutt. "It'll be a cold day in hell when a fool like you can talk that way to me! Go ahead! Try pullin' one of them guns — or both of 'em! Makes no difference to me! You're as good as dead anyway!"

Blinking incredulously, Stretch mumbled a rebuke.

"Aw, c'mon now, that's loco. What's the matter with this town?" The sore-headed cowpokes had picked themselves up and were sidling clear, wincing. "Don't you know lynchin' ain't legal — and gunfightin's unhealthy? Man could get killed."

"No more back-talk, saddlebum!" snarled Button. "I'm givin' you the same chance I gave Pooley! Make your play — or back down!"

19

Stretch shook his head sadly. Shifting his gaze for a few moments, he confirmed his own worst fears. So much for his determination to move in and out of this town quickly and without complications. So much for his distaste for notoriety. All along the street, people watch from doorways and windows. He, the most self-effacing trouble-shooter ever to quit Texas, was now the centre of attention, well and truly in the spotlight. He looked at his challenger again and grimaced in disgust.

"I don't draw on any hothead that hollers 'draw'," he declared.

"You hear that?" Button called to his colleagues. "Just like I thought! Too yellow to stand against me!"

"Who — me?" frowned Stretch. "Well, no. I don't reckon I'm yellow. But I don't draw 'cept to defend myself. So, if you're all that hot for a shootout . . . " He gestured resignedly. "You make the first move."

"So-long, tall man," jeered Button.

"By sundown, you'll be fillin' a six-foot hole!"

With that, he began the fast draw that had won him a big reputation in Keever County. The pearl-butted Colt was clearing leather at bedazzling speed but, by then, Stretch's lefthand .45 was out and booming and the cry of agony erupting from Button was the most harrowing sound heard hereabouts in a month of Sundays. The bullet broke his arm and the impact drove him backward to sprawl in the dust. That flashy pistol, nickel-plated as well as pearl-butted, thudded to the dust beside him. It suddenly occurred to Stretch he had only one chance of deterring Button's friends and admirers. Shock tactics.

His Colt roared again and Button's fancy weapon skittered away crazily. He emptied his other holster and got off three more shots and chilled the blood of three Diamond Seven waddies. They loosed oaths as the well-aimed slugs carried their hats away.

"Now you got to say somethin'," Stretch reminded himself. "And you got to say it right."

Assuming a threatening expression, he delivered his ultimatum.

"I'll aim some lower — less you jaspers clear the street. Go on now! Take your gun-happy buddy to a doctor and then get outa here — muy pronto!"

Nobody heard his sigh of relief. He was being obeyed with alacrity. Perforated Stetsons were hastily retrieved and the wailing, cursing Johnny Button helped to his feet and hustled away. In less than a minute, there were no cowhands in sight. Only the gaping townfolk and the elated mayor, banker and preacher bearing down on the hero of the moment, taking his arms, hustling him up the steps to the porch where the girl waited.

Stretch was at first oblivious to the civic leaders. The girl was searching his homely visage with those wistful brown eyes of hers and he was her

22

slave, slack-jawed, tongue-tied.

"Inside — inside . . . !" Keele was urging. "Hurry, fellers, for the love of Mike. Reverend, shut the door. And you'd better lock and bar it too."

In a daze, Stretch allowed them to force him into the swivel-chair behind the paper-littered desk. It wasn't the tidiest law office he had ever seen, and the bulky, stubbled, unkempt character sleeping drunk on the sagging couch added to the general run-down effect. The girl stood with her back to the cellblock entrance, her eyes still on him. Quinn was positioned at the front window, apprehensively surveying the street. Looking just as apprehensive, the Reverend Abner Wallace hovered by the street-door while the mayor paced excitedly.

Keele's mode of speech was fast and jerky. He introduced himself and his companions, also the girl. Libby Gregg, sister of the jailhouse's only prisoner.

"Reverend Wallace — he's Episcopal — and Tom Quinn of the Quinn Trust

Bank. What do we call you, mister?"

Stretch offered his full name and braced himself for the usual reaction, but it was at once obvious these people had never heard of him. How about that? Just this once, he had happened on a community ignorant of the reputation of the Lone Star Trouble-Shooters.

"I'll make this short, Woody my friend," Keele said briskly. "In case you haven't guessed, we have a bad situation here. Matter of fact the worst crisis this town has ever faced. The prisoner, young Libby's brother Ezra, clobbered Dacey Hargrove in a fist-fight — which Dacey prodded him into. Unfortunately, Dacey's head hit a wall and he never regained consciousness. The funeral was yesterday. Ezra is part of the farming community of Council Valley and the father of the deceased, Rand Hargrove, is the richest and most influential of the cattlemen of Verde Flats, so now we're up against the possibility of a shooting war between cattlemen and farmers."

"Elroy Pooley's deputies lost their nerve and fled right after Ezra's arrest," offered the banker. "And you saw how long Pooley lasted." He nodded to the couch. "That's Newt Cobb. He became county jailer after he abandoned his old trade. Used to be a blacksmith."

"Same time he quit blacksmithing and became turnkey here, he also became an enthusiastic drunk," Keele said in disgust. "Up until then, the damn fool was temperance."

"He was disappointed in love," shrugged Quinn.

"Now here's the proposition, Woody," said Keele. "We'll pin Pooley's badge on you and swear you in and I guarantee my aldermen friends, my fellow-councilmen, will agree to pay you the highest salary ever earned by a lawman in this territory."

Stretch finally found his voice.

"Now — just a doggone minute, gents . . . !"

"I'm talking about a hundred dollars," said Keele. "And I don't mean per month. I mean per week."

"He's worth it," opined Quinn. "The way he overpowered those Diamond Seven thugs . . . "

"The way he uses his guns!" enthused Keele.

"I couldn't wear no tin star," protested Stretch. "It wouldn't be right."

"What's the matter?" challenged Keele. "You aren't wanted by the law of any other territory, are you? Listen, don't worry about it. We don't care what you are. We're desperate, Woody."

"You're our only hope," Quinn pointed out. "If young Gregg is dragged out of here and lynched by cattlemen, Keever County will never be the same. We have a cattle and farming community here, you see."

"Dacey's death turned Keever into a powder-keg with a short fuse," declared Keele. "Ezra's death . . . "

"Dear Lord — no . . . " breathed Libby.

" . . . would touch fire to the fuse," continued Keele. "The whole county would explode."

"Farmhands raiding the Verde Flats ranches," nodded Quinn. "Cattlemen stampeding their herds all across Council Valley, trampling crops."

"You have to consider our position, Woody," begged Keele.

"And the innocents," Wallace solemnly intoned. "Women and children, the families of cattlemen and farmers . . . "

"Caught in the crossfire," muttered Keele.

"Don't I get to say anything?" frowned Stretch.

"By all means," shrugged Keele. "But say it fast. Then I'll swear you in and . . . "

"I ain't wanted by the law anyplace," announced Stretch. "But I ain't no hire-out gunslinger neither. I'm just a peace-lovin' Texan with an itch to wander and — and to mind my own business. Only reason I came to Keever was to buy supplies. My horse is tied outside the emporium along the street a ways. I was all set to ride out — when I saw them waddies crowdin' the little lady . . . "

"The little lady's beggin' for her brother's life, Mister Emerson," murmured Libby. She moved to the desk and started Stretch's pulse racing by placing a hand on his arm. "Poor Ezra never meant to hurt anybody — let alone kill a man. But Dacey Hargrove's dead sure enough, and Ezra'd never try to get away. Even if my pa wanted to break him out of jail, Ezra wouldn't go. He wants his chance to defend himself at a regular trial. That's all he asks."

"But there'll be no trail for him," warned Keele, "unless you can hold him here, Woody."

"Keep the cattlemen at bay," nodded Quinn.

"For less than two weeks," offered Wallace. "The circuit judge is expected on the fifteenth. That's only twelve days away."

"Please," Libby said softly. "Us

Greggs set our minds to it. We know Ezra'll be sent to prison, but we can bear it and so can he. What we can't bear is — him bein' hung with no trial!"

"One good man could do it," muttered Keele. "Front and rear doors locked and barred. Window barricaded. You'll have all the authority that comes with the badge, but we won't expect you to walk patrol or break up riots in any other part of town. We'll make sure you don't go hungry, believe me."

"Every cafe-owner in Keever has refused to deliver meals," Quinn reminded him. "They fear reprisals from the cattlemen. The Hargrove influence is far-reaching, Billy."

"Woody'll have everything he needs," insisted Keele. "We could fill a cell with provisions — enough to last the whole twelve days or more. The stove works, Woody, and there's a well and a privy in the jailhouse yard. All we're asking you to do is sit tight, take good care of your prisoner till the trial."

Right now, Stretch was bedeviled by a fenced-in, deeply-committed feeling. He didn't want any part of this emergency, the badge least of all, being as allergic to symbols of authority as his fiercely independent sidekick. Holy Hannah! If Larry could see him now! He could say no to the mayor, the banker and the preacher, but couldn't say no to the raven-haired girl with the rosy cheeks and the appealing brown eyes. It was that simple. He wouldn't be leaving this town for at least 12 days, maybe longer.

As though reading his mind, Keele offered an assurance.

"Woody, listen if you won't take the job on a permanent basis, let's call it a temporary arrangement."

"You sayin' you won't try to hold me after Ezra has his day in court?" asked Stretch.

"I have this old buddy in Petrie, Arkansas," explained Keele. "We correspond regularly and I'm pretty sure I can persuade him to make the journey, re-settle here and accept the position of county sheriff. He's an experienced peace officer, quite famous in that area. Bob Corlaine. Ever hear of him?" Stretch shook his head. "Well, in Arkansas and Missouri he's a big name. Almost as tall as you, Woody. Big, tough, strong-nerved and expert with every kind of firearm, the kind of lawman no hothead would dare antagonize."

"Too bad he ain't here right now," sighed Stretch.

"He's a native Californian and not all that partial to Arkansas," said Keele. "I'm sure he'll jump at the chance and, by golly, I'll write him this very day, make sure my letter travels on the next stage bound southeast. So, you see, you don't have to feel trapped, stuck here forever. Why, you could be on your way again the day after the trial. But, Woody, it'll take time, you know?"

"Even if Marshal Corlaine left Arkansas the day your letter arrived," said Quinn, "he'd need most of the twelve days to travel to Nevada."

"Woody — I can call you Woody, can't I?" murmured Libby. "Woody, you'd be savin' the life of a good man and — us Greggs'd never forget you for it. Specially me."

"If that young man dies at the hands of a lynch-mob, we have all failed," Wallace said grimly. "It will mean my parishioners have turned their backs on the Lord Almighty. It will mean the end of law and order in Keever County, the end of justice and respect for human life." He added a warning. "And Satan will be well pleased."

"Now, Woody, what can you say to *that* kind of argument?" challenged the mayor.

"Well . . . " Stretch shrugged helplessly. "Maybe just long enough to get your man to court and back."

He was shocked by his own words. Had he really said it? Hell, yes. Banker Quinn was dusting off the badge abandoned by the demoralized Elroy Pooley, the preacher was proffering his bible — and the mayor was ordering him to stand up and raise his right hand.

2

W. E. Emerson, County Sheriff

BY noon of that day, not one of Stretch Emerson's best days, a great formidable quantity of canned goods, eggs, bacon, dried apples and other foodstuffs had been fetched by the mayor, the banker and the preacher and were filling the cell nearest the jailhouse entrance. The civic leaders had gone their way, Keele to arrange the replacement of the shingle bearing Pooley's name, the banker to return to his place of business, the preacher to retire to his church to offer prayers for the survival of the prisoner — also the new sheriff.

The new sheriff finished tidying up, squatted uneasily in the chair behind the desk and considered his predicament. His horse was stabled, his sheathed Winchester, packroll and saddle-bags stashed beside the couch where the jailer still slept, snoring. Figuring he would need all the help of which Newt Cobb was capable, Stretch had carefully collected every bottle he could find and locked them in the bottom righthand drawer of the desk. The street seemed quiet. He had been told Johnny Button was headed back to Diamond Seven with his cohorts after treatment by Dr Myron Sharman, the county's only medico. But, of course, more cattlemen would be coming in, pounding into town to demand the release of the hapless Ezra Gregg for the purpose of making him chief guest at a necktie party.

"Let's see now," he mused, as he ejected his spent shells and reloaded his Colts. "Booze is all locked away. I could stoke up the stove and fix myself some grub any time now. Three shotguns and four Winchesters in the gunrack. I checked the lock on the street-door and it works fine. Uh huh.

Best check the rear door — and I guess I ought to take a look at my prisoner."

He was remembering Libby's grateful smile while taking the keyring from its peg. Before leaving, she had been let into the jail for a brief visit with her brother. That warming, radiant smile, the memory of it, convinced him he had done the right thing, though he was by no means convinced Larry would agree.

On an afterthought, about to unlock the cellblock door, he paused to frown at the befuddled jailer. Did Cobb carry his own set of keys? Best check on that. Until he sobered up, Cobb could not be allowed to carry keys. The implication was obvious — not to mention ominous. If the jailer revived while he was in the cellblock, awakening with a raging thirst, he might let himself out, wander off to the nearest saloon and leave the street-door open for all the lynch-minded cattlemen of Keever County to come barging in.

"You're gettin' smart," he complimented himself. "Startin' to use your brains."

He went to the couch. Cobb snored on while he rolled him over. Sure enough, the second key-ring was secured to the burly man's pants-belt. He unhitched it and, for a few moments, studied the face and physique of this dedicated tippler. Easy to believe he had been a blacksmith. Big feller. Brawny. And the face? Maybe this wasn't the right time for a character analysis. Cobb's heavy-featured visage was blotchy and in need of shaving. The brows were shaggy, the nose bulbous, the mouth broad. So Newt Cobb had been disappointed in love? Maybe he had expected too much. A hombre so ugly setting his cap for an eligible spinster?

He unlocked and entered the cellblock, passed the cell where the provisions were stored and moved on toward the rear door. En route and from the side of his mouth, he drawled a greeting to the jail's only prisoner; Ezra Gregg occupied a cell half-way along.

"Howdy there. Be with you in a minute."

The rear door was strong, its lock in good working order. He raised the bar, set it aside, found the right key and turned it in the lock. Left hand on Colt's butt, he pulled the door open to survey the jailhouse yard. The high fence bordering it was of the stockade type. The well was only a few feet from the door, the privy and ablution-block a short distance away. He was relieved to note the yard contained no gallows.

The prisoner called to him.

"While you got that door open, I need to go out there."

"The privy or the wash-house?" asked Stretch.

"Both," said Ezra Gregg. "Cleanliness is next to godliness, my folks always say."

Stretch ambled to the cell to trade stares with the farm-boy, a husky

20-year-old with a shock of hair as dark as his sister's, a guileless expression and a rueful grin. He wore a rough flannel shirt, moleskin pants and the thick-soled work boots of the typical farmhand.

"Ain't seen you before," he remarked. "You'd be the new sheriff, huh? Libby told me about you. I heard all the ruckus out front. Scared Sheriff Pooley off, did they?"

"He ain't sheriff no more," Stretch said dolefully. "I got stuck with this doggone star."

"'Scuse me for sayin' it," offered Ezra. "You don't look like you're enjoyin' the job."

"Ain't my style," complained Stretch.

"'Tendin' cattle's your style," guessed Ezra. "Yeah. You got the look of a cattleman. So how come you took the job of keepin' me alive for my trial, me that killed a rancher's son?"

Stretch decided against confiding his chief reason — the big brown eyes of Ezra's sister.

"I don't hold with lynchin' is all," he shrugged.

"Well . . . " Again that rueful grin. "That sure makes two of us, Sheriff."

"Am I gonna have trouble with you?" asked Stretch, as he began unlocking the celldoor.

"No trouble at all," Ezra earnestly assured him. "You got my word on that. If I broke out of here, what good would it do? I'd be shot full of holes by the first ranch-hand caught sight of me. I got to have my trial. That's the only way I'll get to say my piece. And the judge, he'll make everybody hush up and listen — even Mister Rand Hargrove himself. Yes, sir. I want to look Mister Hargrove straight in the eye when I tell how I was forced into that fight."

"Let's go," grunted Stretch.

Ezra spent 15 minutes in the privy and 3 in the ablution shack and was then returned to his cell. Not for one second did Stretch relax his vigilance but, for all the trouble the prisoner

40

gave him, he might as well have let him go out there alone. Well, maybe he was too trusting to ever be a reliable lawman.

Before returning to the office, he put a question to Ezra. Had he heard any talk about Newt Cobb, about the big disappointment that had driven him to drink?

"Oh, sure, I got it from Mister Yerby, the barber," nodded Ezra. "Workin' on the farm, I don't get to town as often as them Verde Flats ranch-hands, but that Mister Yerby is some talker and knows everybody else's business."

Thus Stretch learned the object of Cobb's affections had been the buxom Beulah Bogardis, a seamstress employed by the proprietress of a ladies emporium on East Main. The blacksmith had courted her the best way he knew how, but all to no avail. She settled for a short courtship, the whirlwind kind, after a well-heeled professional gambler caught her eye. The happy couple were wed by a

41

justice of the peace, after which they went to California and Cobb went to pieces, sold his business, and became the hardest drinking jailer this county ever had.

"He don't even enjoy all that hard liquor, they say," remarked Ezra. "Throws up all the time."

Stretch winced and declared, "Good booze or cheap rotgut — that's no way to treat it."

"He ain't gonna be much help, huh?" asked Ezra.

"Not with his belly full of booze," shrugged Stretch. "Sober, he might be useful. I'll be seein' you, Ezra. Better fix us some lunch now."

When he returned to the office, Newt Cobb was off the couch and fossicking, mumbling to himself. He ignored the tall stranger at first, being more intent on checking the shelf by the stove and rummaging in the grub-box. The mumbling changed to a clearly-voiced, impatient complaint.

"I didn't use all that last bottle. Got

to be a drink around here someplace."

"You're through with the hard stuff," Stretch said apologetically.

He perched on a corner of the desk as the burly jailer turned to stare at him.

"Who the hell're *you*?"

"Name of Emerson," said Stretch.

"New deputy?"

"New sheriff. Mayor Keele done swore me in a little while ago. Diamond Seven waddies spooked Pooley. He quit."

"Where's my whiskey?"

"Where you can't get at it." As Cobb glowered ferociously and bunched his fists, Stretch tried wheedling. "Don't get mad, Newt. Better if we get along, get to be buddies, you know?"

"If I ain't tastin' whiskey inside a minute, it's gonna cost you some teeth!" scowled Cobb.

"Now, Newt, act reasonable," begged Stretch. "You know the deputies quit too. That leaves just you and me — and a booze-blind turnkey is no help at

43

all. Every cattleman in this territory is hollerin' for Ezra's blood. They're hot to lynch. So — doggone it — you and me have to stay sharp-eyed and clear-headed."

"I get a drink — right *now* . . . " raged Cobb. "Or I tear you apart!"

Stretch slid from the desk and braced himself. The big man lumbered at him, telegraphing a swing, a wild blow that would have hurled him all the way to the side wall had it connected. With genuine regret, he parried it and threw a short jab to Cobb's face. Cobb recoiled, blinked dazedly and said, "Oh, hell. I sure felt that."

His legs buckled. He crumpled to the floor and, for a few moments, mumbled curses and groaned and clasped calloused hands to his head as though fearful it were about to fall off. With some effort, he regained his feet. It being obvious threats would not achieve his purpose, he tried pleading. Stretch sadly shook his head.

"But I *gotta* have a drink!" wailed

Cobb. "Bein' sober is pure misery. 'Less I'm drunk, I start thinkin' of *her* again — pinin' for her! It ain't *human* what you're doin' to me!"

"Can't do it, Newt," said Stretch. "Need you on your feet and fit for your chores. I'm real sorry about Beulah Bogardis, but you just got to get used to her bein' wed to another man. And now you're gonna help me fix us some grub. Prisoner's hungry and so am I — and you ought to eat somethin'."

"I couldn't eat a damn thing!" gasped Cobb.

But, some 45 minutes later, he was wolfing his share of the humble repast rustled up by his new boss, slabs of beef cooked in tomatoes and chili. He grudgingly agreed to keep an eye on the coffeepot while Stretch toted a laden platter in to the prisoner and, in due course, he swigged two cups of coffee, hot and black.

"This ain't gonna do you no good," he warned. "If you think I'll side a lawman that hid my liquor, you're crazier'n you look. You're some ugly hombre — you know that?"

"You and me — two of a kind, Newt," shrugged Stretch. "no offense, but purty you ain't."

He threw another fistful of coffee into the pot, filled it with water and set it on the stove. Cobb bestired himself to the extent of shoving more wood into the fire. They brewed and drank coffee, Stretch wondering how many more hours would pass before an irate and derisive Larry arrived in Keever, Cobb wondering how long he would last on nought but coffee.

Another cattleman had come to town at about the time the county jailer roused from his drunken slumber. Jerry Floren, boss of the Broken Arrow spread, was the only local rancher grazing a herd away from Verde Flats; his outfit was located less than a quarter-mile north of Council Valley, centre of the farming community of which Marvin Gregg was unofficial leader. Sharp-featured and garbed in expensive range clothes, Floren arrived quietly, expecting to see Main Street thronged, ranch-hands from other spreads storming the jailhouse. He made straight for the office of Arnold Rossiter, the most notable of Keever's resident lawyers, notable for having become a suitor for the hand of the beautiful Selma Hargrove, daughter of the all-powerful Diamond Seven boss.

Rossiter was in pensive mood when Floren entered his office without knocking and helped himself to a chair. Well-groomed and handsome, distinguished-looking, he was generally regarded as the ideal choice for a lady as eligible, as highly-educated as the fair Selma, though nobody had ascertained Selma's attitude in the matter.

Floren scorned greetings and bluntly remarked, "I thought it'd be over by now."

"I too." frowned the lawyer. "From where I was watching, it seemed Johnny

47

Button and his roughneck friends would have their way."

"You'd better tell me what happened, cousin," urged Floren.

Rossiter promptly chided him.

"You have a poor memory, Jerry. We mutually agreed we should keep our relationship a secret — remember?"

"Whatever you say," shrugged Floren. "Well?"

"The unexpected sometimes happens," said Rossiter. "Pooley took fright when Button challenged him to a gun-duel . . ."

"Pooley would," grinned Floren. "Always was weak-bellied."

"But no sooner had Pooley fled than a stranger butted in," said Rossiter. "Just a saddletramp, I'd say, very little intelligence, but very much the man of action. Three Diamond Seven riders were manhandling Ezra's sister, who showed up at the inopportune moment. The stranger got the better of them, was challenged by Button and then proceeded to demonstrate his gun-skill.

A two-gun man, if you please."

"You telling me he backed Button down?" frowned Floren.

"Broke Button's gunarm with his first bullet," said Rossiter. "Temporarily discouraged the others by shooting their hats off."

"Hey, that's quite a trick," muttered Floren.

"Very flashy I thought," said Rossiter. "But the lynch party was suitably impressed, and so were Billy Keele and his friends."

"Oh." Floren nodded knowingly. "Quinn and the preacher. Them again."

"They made short work of installing the stranger as sheriff," said Rossiter. "His name is Emerson. Ever hear of him?"

"Don't know him — don't much care about him," drawled Floren. "This is just a delay, Arnie. It'll take more than one gunslinger and a whiskey-head jailer to hold off every waddy in the country. The Gregg kid won't last till the judge

49

arrives, not with Rand and McNear breathing fire, demanding vengeance for Dacey. Wouldn't surprise me if Rand posts bounty on Ezra. He's grieving, you know? Dacey was the apple of his eye."

"The other son too," Rossiter assured him. "And Selma — though Rand and his daughter have little in common nowadays." He grinned satirically. "It's more than mere grief, Jerry. The old man's pride is outraged, his sense of superiority."

"So it'll happen sure enough," opined Floren. "With McNear putting the spur into him, old Rand's just bound to make war on the Council Valley crowd. There'll be raiding parties moving into the valley after the lynching. They'll be run out, Arnie. Every last sodbuster."

"The sooner the better," said Rossiter.

"Only a matter of time," Floren said confidently. "A week at most."

★ ★ ★

It was 3 p.m. when Ernie Griff, a stablehand whose favorite pastime was tale-carrying, reached Diamond Seven on a borrowed horse. Impressive it was, the headquarters of the county's most prosperous rancher, a fine double-storied ranch-house, hacienda-style, occupied pride of place, a home surrounded by well-kept gardens tended by a small army of Mexican servants, a home designed for gracious living. Surveying it for the first time, a shrewd observer would recognize it for what it was, a monument to the drive, the bull-headedness and enterprise of a cattleman who had come up the hard way. So strong was the Hargrove work force, it took two bunkhouses to accommodate his herders. And there were three barns, a storehouse, countless outhouses and a whole network of corrals in sight of the palatial Hargrove home.

Griff blurted out his news to the foreman, brawny, heavy-featured Burch McNear, who had been Hargrove's partner way back when the first Diamond Seven herd was driven onto Verde Flats. Some years younger than the cattle baron, McNear was respected as the county's most experienced ramrod, and the toughest. Having heard all the gossip-monger had to say, he tossed him a coin and dismissed him, then made for the shaded front porch of the ranch-house where Rand Hargrove awaited him.

Spare of physique, weatherbeaten and balding, his ash-grey spade beard matching the tufts at his temples, Hargrove was slumped in his rocking chair, brooding, still plagued by grief and hot indignation, burning resentment of the Council Valley community. From his surviving son, the arrogant and wayward Chuck, he could count on eager agreement to any proposed action against the farmers. From his wife and daughter, he had to suffer what he now interpreted as disloyalty. Sophie Hargrove had been raised in this territory, the daughter of Keever's first Western Union representative. The sons of this marriage had inherited their father's aggressive nature. Only Selma had inherited Sophie's looks; at the time of her marriage to Rand Hargrove, she was the county's most sought-after beauty, an outstandingly attractive 18-year-old, allergic to violence.

Mother and daughter emerged from the house as McNear climbed to the porch. He bared his thatch of dark hair, nodded to them, then squatted on the porch-rail and relayed the news.

"The saddletramp that wounded Johnny Button — they pinned the star on him and swore him in."

"Billy Keele's idea," guessed Hargrove. "That two-bit do-gooder."

"With Johnny he got lucky," McNear said grimly. "You say the word, Rand, and I'll take the whole outfit in. Flyin' W and Bar Ten'll throw in with us — and how's one gun gonna hold out against so many? We'll have Dacey's killer by sundown."

"Burch, I don't understand how you

can talk this way," protested Hargrove's wife. She was still a good-looking woman and McNear was well aware of it. Not too many lines in the appealing, oval-shaped face. The fair hair only slightly grey-flecked. The figure still slender. "To hang a man without trial is murder. There's no other word for it."

"Our eldest is dead, woman," scowled Hargrove. "Murdered by a sodbuster's son."

Selma now spoke up and, not for the first time, Hargrove found himself bitterly regretting having sent her to the west coast to round off her education. Too much study, he was wont to complain, too much learning for any woman. She had graduated top of her class, achieving honors in subjects he had never heard of and could never understand; what the hell was psychology anyway?

"Be reasonable in your grief, Dad," she urged. "Try to see this tragedy from the Gregg boy's side of it. Can you claim he meant to kill Dacey? A farm-boy defending himself in a brawl with a Hargrove — with intent to murder? No Keever jury will accept that. And Judge Mayo will probably call it manslaughter — perhaps accidental death."

"I reckon your father knows what to expect from the law, Miss Selma," muttered McNear. "Justice for Ezra Gregg — but not for Dacey. If we don't act fast, that sodbuster's whelp might never be punished."

"An eye for an eye," growled Hargrove. "He has to pay, damn him!"

"For this, you helped Keever's first lawmen run the outlaws out of this territory?" Selma challenged. "To make Keever safe for the law-abiding? Or to attain so much power, so much influence, that you could take the law into your own hands?"

He glowered at her, remembering the spindly 10-year-old who, for a brief period of her development, promised to become a tomboy. That 10-year-old had been easy to handle. This

55

imperious blonde beauty, of age now, was like a foreigner to him nothwithstanding the striking resemblance to Sophie. She had poise and grace and, with a single look, could make him feel inadequate. For that, could he ever forgive her?

"This ain't the big city," he pointed out. "This is still the frontier, Miss High-And-Mighty, and you better believe that. Unless I take care of the man that butchered my son, all them valley farmers'll say I'm too weak to stand against 'em."

"Next thing we know, Verde Flats ranchers'll be losin' stock," McNear predicted. "There'll be farmhands sneakin' north to steal cattle."

"That's not so, Burch," chided Sophie. "Until Dacey's death, there was never any trouble except for a few brawls in town when cattlemen and farmhands swapped insults. The trouble was never serious and there were never any thefts. While ever the valley men stay the flats, while ever cattlemen stay clear of the valley, we could all have peace. Why, the valley is a full three miles from here."

"Marvin Gregg's people have never disputed cattlemens' claims to Verde Flats," Selma pointed out. "Why then should you resent their farming the Council Valley?"

"They can't stay," her father said curtly. "Sooner or later, I'm gonna have to drive every last sodbuster out of the county. Should've done it years ago. Then Dacey'd still be alive — 'stead of buried in the county cemetery."

"Not true!" Selma protested. "In the name of sanity, Dad, think with your brain, not with your emotions!"

"If you two got no objection, I have to talk private with my foreman," said Hargrove.

The women traded glances and withdrew into the house. McNear lit a cigar and eyed the rancher expectantly.

"All you got to do is say the word," he offered.

"Well . . . " Hargrove shrugged uncomfortably. "There's plenty time. Ain't as if Judge Mayo's gonna arrive tomorrow."

"You gettin' squeamish?" challenged McNear. "Hell, Rand, you got any idea how *I* feel? I helped raise Dacey, don't forget. Held him on my knee when he was just a little sprig . . . "

"All right, Burch," sighed Hargrove. "All right."

"Said you'd run every sodbuster out, didn't you?" growled McNear. "So? Are we just gonna talk about it?"

"I want Gregg to suffer the way I'm sufferin'," muttered Hargrove. "That smart-schooled daughter of mine, Burch, she said one thing makes sense. I shouldn't just think of how *I'm* feelin'? Well . . . " He grinned coldly. "Now I'm wonderin' how Gregg feels right now."

"You mean that young whelp in the county jail?" frowned McNear.

"I mean his father," said Hargrove. He talked on and, by his words, proved how little he understood of the attitudes of the boss-farmer of Council Valley. "He'll spook pretty soon, I figure. Scared his boy's gonna be dragged out of that calaboose and strung up. So what d'you suppose he'll do? My guess is he'll rally a couple dozen sodbusters and try a raid — and get his fool head blowed off."

"Unless this Emerson feller sides with the sodbusters," warned McNear.

"Emerson was sworn in by Billy Keele," countered Hargrove. "And we know Keele don't dare side with one bunch or the other. We've heard Keele make the same damn speech at every election with Quinn and the sin-killer backin' him up. A square deal for all, he always says. The Keever administration works for cattlemen, townfolk and farmers alike. The democratic way is what he calls it. That's Keele's policy and he's stuck with it and, if Emerson hopes to earn what they're payin' him, he has to go along. He'll turn his guns on a jailbreak party as fast as he'd shoot at a lynch-mob." He chuckled harshly. "So maybe ol' psalm-singin' Marv Gregg is gonna learn how it feels to bleed and hurt and die."

"I still say we ought to hit that jailhouse with everything," growled McNear. "That's what we owe Dacey."

"I don't need you to tell me what I owe my son," retorted Hargrove. And then he asked, "Where's my other boy? What've you done with Chuck?"

"Him and a couple others, I sent 'em to man our north lineshack," said the ramrod. "Hangin' around here was bad for him, Rand. Kept remindin' him of his brother. I figured it'd be easier on him, sendin' him up to Red Rock Ridge." He hesitated a moment before voicing an accusation. "You've always been the boss — until now."

Hargrove's eyes gleamed.

"We've been together a long time, Burch," he said softly. "I guess that gives you a right to speak your mind. But — you better explain what you just said."

"*You* answer *my* question," urged McNear. "When the time comes, who's gonna decide about bustin' that killer out of jail and hangin' him? You — or the women?"

Through clenched teeth, Hargrove mumbled a warning.

"You leave Sophie and the girl to me, understand? Just — leave 'em to me."

McNear grimaced impatiently, slid from the rail and quit the porch, leaving the cattle baron to his brooding.

At sundown, Larry squatted by his fire and morosely studied the contents of the sizzling pan. His supper would be meagre. He anticipated his belly would begin growling again within an hour of eating. And no coffee! And he had smoked the last vestiges of his Bull Durham an hour ago. What had become of the beanpole?

"Damn pea-brained stringbean should've got back hours ago," he grouched, and so bitter was his mood that the sorrel sensed it, nickered uneasily and stared his way. "What the hell're *you* gawkin' at?" he challenged the animal. "You're feedin' on sweet grass and you got plenty to drink, so you should complain?"

He craved coffee — generously spiked with rye whiskey. Another creature comfort, one he regarded as his right, was being denied him, thanks to his partner's continued absence.

Never once did it occur to him Stretch might be in danger, laid up with a mortal wound maybe. Since their first meeting as gangling teenagers, enlisting in the Confederate Cavalry, since their first taste of combat, he had regarded Stretch as indestructible and over-endowed with what they had come to define as Lone Star Luck. If in Keever some rowdy had taken a swing at Stretch's jaw, that rowdy would now be nursing skinned knuckles and a broken nose and the Emerson jaw would be none the worse for the experience. If some homicidal local had taken a shot at Stretch he had missed at best or, at worst inflicted a minor wound and was now being laid out for burial. Stretch was a survivor by instinct. Larry took this for granted. He wasn't worrying about his partner. He was heaping curses on him, assuming he had been arrested for disturbing the peace and was now sitting snug in jail.

"And bein' fed regular," mused Larry. "while I set here near starvin'."

He had tried fishing the creek. The fish just weren't jumping. In the late afternoon he had saddled up for a hunting expedition. Same result. No game in sight, not as much as one scrawny jackrabbit or an elderly, slow-off-the-ground quail. And so he simmered and cursed and came to a decision.

"I give you till sun-up, stringbean. Then I'm comin' in for you. And heaven help you when I find you!"

The meagre supper was less than satisfactory. He rolled into his blanket to sleep and was soon resenting his reliance on tobacco. Smoking was a damn fool habit anyway, but oh how he craved the makings right now. No coffee. No whiskey, No tobacco. How would he make it through the night?

He slept fitfully and came awake at sunrise — hungry and mean. Why had he used up the last of his food for last night's supper? There was so little of it, not enough for one square meal and certainly not enough for two. He drank creek-water, saw to his horse and refilled his canteen, then shaved and bathed, donned his clothing, strapped on his Colt and gathered his gear. He had one thought in mind as he saddled up for the ride to the county seat. If he met any other travelers this side of Keever, he would beg a smoke. If begging didn't work, he would offer to pay — any price.

"You can take care of yourself, huh?" He thought of his partner again as he rode through the hills. "Don't need for me to nursemaid you every mile you travel? *That'll* be the day! Get ready to hang your dumb head in shame, stringbean! Get ready to eat crow! You had the consarn gall to cuss me out. Real proddy you turned. Well — damn your saddlesore hide — when I get my hands on you . . . !"

He had not reached the east fringe of the hills when he spotted the approaching horsemen, four of them, and heaved a sigh of relief. Oh, brother. Hired hands from some Keever County ranch? Why, they might even be carrying jerky or some other edibles, might even have a bottle. And they would never deny him a smoke.

As they drew closer, he noted their attire and realized they would never herd cattle. Farmhands. Sodbusters for sure. But never mind. He bore no grudge against farmers.

The farmhands, a small hunting party from Council Valley, were venturing into the hills in hopes of downing a deer or two. Now, they followed the approach of the lone rider as intently as he followed theirs.

"Cowhand," one of them observed bitterly.

"And all by himself," growled another. "So now it's our turn, huh Dade?"

"Our turn to prove no show-off cattleman's any better'n a farmer," the burly Dade agreed.

"He's wavin' to us," another man noted, puffing on a corncob pipe. "Actin' real friendly."

"That ain't gonna help him," scowled Dade. "Not one little bit."

3

Another Texan In Town

THE hunters reined up. Larry reined up beside them and worked up an amiable grin, greeting them cordially.

"'Mornin', fellers. Sure glad I ran into you."

"You are, huh?" challenged Dade, running a scathing eye over him.

Though they hadn't worked cattle in quite a time, the drifters had never abandoned the type of clothing in which they were most comfortable, the rough shirts and bandanas, the sweat-stained Stetsons, vest, denim jackets, Levis and batwing chaps of the typical Texas range rider.

"Out of everything," Larry explained. "Sent my partner to Keever for supplies and, doggone him, he's still there. So

67

I didn't eat this mornin' and, worst of all, I had my last smoke last night — before supper?" He appealed to them. "Can any of you oblige me with the makin's?"

"How d'you like that?" jeered Dade. "A damn, stinkin' cow-poke — tryin' to beg a smoke from the likes of us."

"We sure don't owe you no favors, cowboy," growled another farmhand. "Guess you Verde Flats gunslicks figure you can get anything you want from us farmhands, huh?"

"I was askin' — polite and friendly," frowned Larry. "And I ain't from Verde Flats, wherever that is. I'm a stranger hereabouts, never was here before."

"You're a cowhand anyway," accused Dade. "A sixgun-packin' show-off cowhand. Old Man Hargrove and them other big shot cattlemen, they don't have gunslingers enough? Hirin' more help to hound us farmhands, are they?"

"Friend, I don't know what you're talkin' about," said Larry.

"And I don't know how you could work up the nerve to face all four of us," retorted Dade.

Larry grinned wryly.

"Friend, it don't take much nerve," he declared, "when a hombre needs a smoke as bad as I do."

"Don't call me that again!" snapped Dade. "Don't call me 'friend'! I'm no friend of any damn cowpoke!"

"Take it easy." Larry's grin faded. "It just happens I'm totin' no grudge against farmers — even soreheads like you. And now, if none of you boys'll oblige me with the makin's, I'll ride on to Keever and buy my own."

"When you get to Keever," growled Dade, "tell everybody it was Dade Bates did this to you!"

His hamlike fist swung hard and fast to Larry's head and, dazed and sore, Larry keeled from his saddle. He thought to draw his boots from stirrups as he went down, flopping beside his sorrel with an impact that jarred every bone and muscle.

Chuckling harshly, Dade dismounted. Another man followed suit and, as Larry rolled over, he saw both of them coming at him. He was rising as Dade aimed a kick at his face.

Throwing himself sideways, heaving himself upright, all his frustration, his need of food, liquor and tobacco got the better of him. He gave up on trying to restrain his temper and, summoning all his muscle-power, lunged at Dade and drove a fist into his face. Dade promptly backstepped, his legs buckling, and the other man attacked from Larry's left side, his big fists pounding. Larry took a left that bloodied his ear, a right that almost sent him down again, then retaliated with a wild uppercut so powerful that his assailant was lifted and thrown three yards. Dust clouds arose when the man hit the ground shoulders-first. Larry whirled and glowered at the other two. One, in the act of dismounting, froze in shock, gaping. Slowly and carefully, he lowered the raised leg and returned boot to stirrup.

Larry cold-eyed the fourth farmhand. That one swallowed a lump in his throat, gestured placatingly and detached the corn-cob from between his teeth, asking, "You wanna smoke my pipe?"

"Keep your pipe," scowled Larry. "I don't want a damn thing from you hothead farm-boys." He retrieved and donned his Stetson and swung into his saddle. "This your idea of peaceful livin'?" he jibed. "Four of you huntin' ranch-hands, hopin' to find one ridin' alone so you can gang up on him?"

"Well, hell, we ain't huntin' cow-hands," the pipe-smoker earnestly assured him. "We're just headed into the hills to hunt deer."

"I didn't find nothin' to hunt," sighed Larry. "That's why I'm headed for Keever with my belly empty."

Without a glance at his prone and groaning adversaries, he heeled the sorrel to speed and resumed his eastward journey. He had been angry when breaking camp. Now he was in a fury, controlling himself with difficulty. The next hot-head who back-talked him, be he farm-boy, ranch-hand or town-man, would be risking life and limb.

He made Keever at 8.15 a.m. his mood incendiary. Spoiling for a fight with his unreliable sidekick, he could not ignore the void within. He needed to eat. Oh. hell! *How* he needed to eat! The proprietor of a hash-house in the first block was sweeping the sidewalk in front of his premises when Larry swung down, looped his rein to the hitchrail and advanced on him.

"Inside!" he ordered.

The cafe-owner was overweight, but found himself hustled into his place of business as easily as if he were a skinny youth.

"I — ain-t worth robbin'!" he panted. "Don't keep much cash around — just change for my trade . . . !"

"Mister, I ain't here to rob you," Larry said grimly. "I'm a customer, savvy? I'm here to eat." He pointed to the kitchen. "So do your doggone duty muy pronto!"

"Yes, *sir*!" gasped the cafe-owner. "Comin' right up. What's your pleasure?"

"*Eatin*'!" snarled Larry.

"I mean — uh — what would you like to eat?"

"Stack of hot biscuits — so high." Larry raised a hand. "Ham and eggs. The ham — it better be thick slabs. And six eggs sunny side up. And coffee, hot and black and strong. *Move!*"

Thirty minutes later, his appetite satisfied, it occurred to him this flabby hash-slinger was a neutral after all. When he approached the counter and dug out his wallet, he remembered his manners.

"Didn't mean to scare the hell out of you, friend," he muttered. "Bein' that hungry is bad for my disposition."

"I noticed," the flabby man dared to assure him.

Larry paid for his breakfast, added a heavy tip and asked the whereabouts of the nearest store. After that meal, his craving for tobacco was stronger still.

"Bartholomew's emporium is just a couple doors along," offered the cafe-owner. "But . . . "

About to turn away, Larry paused.

"But what?"

"Don't scare Cy Bartholomew, huh?" pleaded the cafe-owner. "He's a nice feller, good friend of mine and one of the gentlest human bein's I know."

"I'll try to remember that," Larry promised.

He led the sorrel to the second hitchrail along, looped his rein again and strode into the store to be greeted by the ageing, balding, ruddy-faced proprietor.

"Morning. What can I show you?"

"Bull Durham, papers, matches," Larry said firmly.

He dropped a coin on the counter and proceeded to roll a much-needed quirley. Bartholomew grinned ruefully as he scratched a match on a thumbnail, lit up and took a long drag.

"I know the feeling," he remarked. "Couple nights back, I couldn't recall where I left my pipe. Took me two hours to find it, and it felt like two weeks."

"How's your memory now?" asked Larry, blowing a smoke-ring.

"It works pretty good," said Bartholomew.

"I'm lookin' for my partner," said Larry. "He's Texan like me and . . ."

"As tall as you?"

"Taller. He's six and a half feet and built like a beanpole, rides a pinto, packs two Colts."

"You'll find him at the county jail," offered Bartholomew.

He recoiled, startled by Larry's violent reaction.

"Where the hell *else*!" scowled Larry. "I should ask such a dumb question? Sure he's at the county jail — him that was so sure he could take care of himself . . ." He turned and made for the entrance. "Didn't need me along, he said. Huh! By himself, he ain't nothin' but trouble! Pea-brained, clumsy, jug-eared jackass . . . "

Before the storekeeper could add relevant details, Larry was out of the store and on his way again, slipping his rein, remounting, barking a demand at a passing local. The local was shabby, dispirited and easily intimidated, Ike Jeffers by name, deadbeat, panhandler and town drunk. Nervously he obeyed Larry's demand, directing him to the county jail.

In the law office, pacing in agitation, full of breakfast but still craving booze, Newt Cobb paused by the window and sighted the approaching rider.

"Whoever this ranch-hand is, he looks mean enough to try tearin' this calaboose apart," he observed. "Ain't sure if he's Diamond Seven or Flyin' W." Watching Larry rein up at the law office hitch-rail, he added, "Ain't sure I ever saw him before."

Stretch winced and retreated to the cellblock entrance. From there he asked, "Built hefty about the shoulders, dark-haired, near as tall as me? Ridin' a sorrel gelding?" Cobb nodded. Stretch winced again and offered advice. "When he pounds on the door, open up fast. He's my partner. Keep him waitin' and he's liable to tear out the lock with his teeth and bust the door with his fists." He moved along to the occupied cell to alert the prisoner. "Ezra, you'll be hearin' some heavy cussin' and a heap of hollerin' any minute now. Just want you to know it won't be another lynch-mob, so you don't need to fret."

He left Ezra frowning perplexedly and returned to the office. Standing in the cellblock entrance, he braced himself and prepared for the inevitable Valentine reaction. The street-door shook from Larry's pounding. Cobb raised the bar and eyed Stretch expectantly. Stretch tossed the keys. Cobb unlocked the door and moved to one side as Larry stormed in.

"You damn no-account . . . !" he raged, advancing on the taller Texan.

"Lock up again, Newt, and throw me them keys," muttered Stretch.

Cobb obeyed, his wary gaze on the incensed newcomer. Right up to Stretch walked Larry, to glare into his face and prod at his chest with an accusing forefinger.

"Don't need me along all the time, huh? You can take care of yourself? Helpless as a half-wit child you are — and twice as useless . . . !"

"Uh — hold on now, runt," pleaded Stretch. "Gimme a chance to explain how I . . . "

"Shuddup while I'm cussin' you!" fumed Larry. "One easy little chore, short ride to the county seat for supplies! You could handle it alone you said. Back by early afternoon. Damn and blast! I could've starved out there!"

"It's thisaway . . . " began Stretch.

"I ain't through cussin'!" snapped Larry.

"'Scuse me," sighed Stretch.

"You left me with nothin'!" bellowed

78

Larry, his finger still prodding. "Scarce anything to eat! No coffee, no booze, no tobacco! Left me with nothin' while you came to this burg and got yourself in another damn mess! Why the hell don't you admit it? You just had to stumble into trouble again and . . . !"

His voice choked off. His prodding finger struck something unyielding, something metallic and, automatically, he lowered his eyes from his partner's troubled face to squint at what Mayor Keele had fixed to his vest. For a long moment he stared uncomprehendingly. He knuckled at his eyes, bent to inspect the badge, shook his head incredulously and loosed a violent oath. Cobb chose that moment to point out. "He's sheriff now."

Larry swore explosively.

"I don't believe it!"

"Pure truth, runt," mumbled Stretch. "But I couldn't help it. Libby was pleadin' and the mayor too and the banker feller and Reverend Wallace . . . "

"It's a joke!" gasped Larry. "They

couldn't mean it!"

"You see, it was thisaway," offered Stretch. "There was these waddies raisin' hell out front, plannin' on bustin' Ezra out of here and stringin' him up. Well, you know we don't hold with lynchin', right? It's somethin' we plumb disapprove of, right? So I had to cool these hotheads that was manhandlin' Libby — she's Ezra's sister — and another waddy tried to draw on me, so I had to discourage him, didn't I?"

"They can't make you sheriff!" cried Larry. "Nobody with a brain in his head is gonna swear in a jackass like you!"

"You better check the sign out front," shrugged Stretch. And, again, he tossed the keys to Cobb, who raised the bar and unlocked the street door. "Go on, runt, Go see for yourself."

In a daze, Larry trudged out to the porch. He descended to the sidewalk, took a deep breath, then turned and raised his eyes to the new shingle, fresh-painted, bright and clear. It read: W. E. Emerson, Sheriff, Keever County, Nevada. His eyes dilated and his jaw sagged. His movements were unsteady as he climbed to the porch and re-entered the office. Cobb re-secured the door and tossed the keys to Stretch. Uneasily, Stretch watched Larry sag into a chair. For a long moment, an awkward silence. Then Larry regained the power of speech.

"They couldn't just lock you up for mixin' into a scrap — like every other time," he muttered. "Oh, no. This time, they swore you in — pinned a tin star on you."

"Same hothead I shot, he spooked the other sheriff," shrugged Stretch. "They didn't have nobody to hold Ezra for the circuit-judge. And Libby kept pleadin' — with them big brown eyes — and I couldn't work up the nerve to refuse 'em."

Larry's hands trembled as he produced his Bull Durham. He began building a smoke — clumsily.

"You better tell it all," he said shakily. "Start from the beginnin'. Don't give me Ezra and his sister with her big brown eyes. I never heard of Ezra. Just let me have it slow and careful, the way it all happened. Make sense. Make me savvy what the hell's goin' on."

While talking, Stretch moved to the chair behind the desk. He was intimidated by Larry's reaction, though that reaction was exactly as he had expected, and now went to pains to explain everything in proper sequence, one point at a time, starting with his arrival in Keever, his purchase of supplies, then going on to recount the violent incidents he had witnessed and the consequences thereof. For 10 minutes he talked, Larry slumped in his chair, smoking, listening intently. The shock was easing, the Valentine brain returning to working order. He said nothing until his partner stopped talking. Then, "That's all?" he challenged.

"Well," said Stretch. "That's the gizzard of it."

"You got no deputies?" prodded Larry. "There's just you and the turnkey — and he'd rather drink himself blind in some saloon than do his duty and sit guard on this Ezra hombre?"

Cobb defended himself earnestly.

"I got rights. Only way I can forget my grief is with booze. If I'm sober, I keep rememberin' her."

Larry turned in his chair, eyes narrowing.

"You keep rememberin' *who*?" he coldly enquired.

"Her," said Cobb.

"Meanin' Beulah Bogardis," explained Stretch. "Lady that hitched up with a sportin' man and vamoosed from this town. Newt's still pinin' for her."

Flushed with fury, Larry glowered at the turnkey.

"You call that a fair reason for soakin' your brain in booze?" he challenged. "Hell! A grown man actin' like some damn chicken-livered kid?" His mouth contorted in disgust. "Disappointed in love. Damn and blast you, what'll it matter when you're dead and gone? How long is a man supposed to pine for the one woman — his whole life? Cobb, you're a damn fool!"

"You mind your mouth, Tex!" gasped Cobb, bunching his fists. "I don't have to take that kind of talk from . . . !"

"You'll take it, like it or not," countered Larry, rising, eyeing him scathingly. "What the hell, Cobb? What happened to your pride? You got important work here. Get drunk again and, while you're hung over, there could be another lynch-mob break the door down, shoot my fool partner full of holes and hang your prisoner right there in the main street! Is that worth a bellyful of booze to a whinin', lovesick jackass like you? If us men're gonna lose our guts every time some female cold-shoulders us, we might's well blow our brains out. We ain't fit to live."

"Easy, runt," begged Stretch.

"Easy nothin'!" flared Larry. "That tin star could be the death of you — and the only help you got is a damn lovesick no-account bellyachin' about some woman that took up with a tinhorn!"

"You got a mean mouth!" breathed Cobb, advancing on him. "And I've been sober since yesterday mornin'! You can mean-talk me when I'm drunk but — when I'm sober — it's gonna cost you!"

He bounded at Larry with a fist drawn back and that fist was still drawn back when he barged into Larry's rock-hard left. The impact jarred Larry's arm from wrist to elbow and made a profound impression on the ex-blacksmith. Backward he stumbled, a livid bruise on his chin, his big fists dangling. He came up hard against the couch, flopped to it, then slid to the floor and, in that squatting posture, shook his head and complained, "You hit hard. By damn, you hit *awful* hard."

"I won't hit you again," Larry said in contempt. "You ain't worth skinnin' my knuckles on." He jerked a thumb and growled a command to Stretch. "Open the door and let him out."

"Well, I don't reckon I ought . . ." began Stretch.

"Let him go," urged Larry. "Let him hotfoot it to the nearest saloon and drown himself in rotgut. It's all he's good for — and he sure ain't any help to you."

"Whatever you say, runt," sighed Stretch.

As he rose and reached for the keyring, Cobb mumbled at him.

"You don't have to turn me loose. Not if I'm stayin'."

"You're stayin'?" blinked Stretch.

"Damn right." The turnkey raised himself to the couch and perched on its edge, a hand clasped to his jaw, his eyes locking with Larry's. "Don't think

I can do it, do you? Don't believe I got the guts to beat my cravin' for booze?"

"Man can do anything he wants," growled Larry.

"Now, Newt, you was temperance before Beulah turned you down and hitched up with that gambler," Stretch pointed out. "It oughtn't be that rough on you, quittin' the hard stuff."

"I can do it," Cobb assured Larry. "You'll see, Texas . . ."

"He's Larry Valentine," offered Stretch. "You can call him Larry, but only if you're gonna stay friendly."

"I'll prove it to you, Larry Valentine," declared Cobb.

"Maybe," shrugged Larry.

"You're gonna hang around and side me, ain't you, runt?" asked Stretch. "Mayor Keele, he'd be right happy to swear you in as deputy and . . ."

He flinched from Larry's venomous glare.

"*Me* wear a badge?"

"It was just an idea," said Stretch.

"I wasn't meanin' to insult you."

"You're a sheriff," Larry reminded him. "It ain't permanent but, while you carry that tin star, you better *think* like a sheriff. The mayor says you should fort up here and I'll allow that makes good sense. But, if I let him swear me in, we'd both be stuck in this jailhouse. One of us has to stay loose — on the outside — movin' around and diggin' into this mess."

"You're good at that," Stretch said admiringly.

"Don't pay me no compliments," scowled Larry.

"So what're you gonna do now?" asked Stretch.

"Talk to your prisoner," decided Larry. "I might's well know what kind of fool sodbuster you're riskin' your hide for."

"Help yourself," nodded Stretch. "But don't bawl him out, Larry, huh? I mean, he's got trouble enough."

Larry strode into the jailhouse, slamming the door behind him. Cobb rose and trudged to the stove to make coffee. Very quietly, he remarked to Stretch.

"Your buddy is quite a man."

"Real rough, real hard," warned Stretch. "Do yourself a favor, Newt. Don't tangle with him again."

"He talks straight," mused Cobb. "Says things right out. Thinks I'm no-account." He sighed heavily and shook his head. "That's bad. I don't like that at all."

"Man gets to be a drunk, there's many'll call him trash," shrugged Stretch.

"I don't care a damn what anybody else calls me," said Cobb. "Only care what Larry says. He's special. The way he looked at me. Hell. I felt like somethin' that crawled out from under a wet rock." He shook his head. "I got to change that. Ain't gonna feel right — about anything — till your buddy gets to respectin' me."

Having inspected the rear door, Larry

moved to Ezra's cell, leaned against the barred door and surveyed him intently. Ezra quit the bunk and came to the door, the better to return Larry's scrutiny.

"'Mornin'." He nodded politely. "You're the sheriff's friend?"

"And you're the scrapper that hit Dacey Hargrove hard enough to kill him," growled Larry.

"Funny about that," frowned Ezra.

"I ain't laughin'," said Larry. "Rand Hargrove ain't laughin'. And every gun on his payroll is against you. So what's funny?"

"Well, I clobbered him, sure," shrugged Ezra. "And he hit a wall head-first, sure. But, you know, it didn't look like he hit it all that hard. Hard enough to knock himself out — but to die of it?" He shook his head slowly. "I still don't savvy that."

"Tell me about it," ordered Larry.

Ezra told it in just a few minutes. He rarely got to visit the county seat. When he did, he allowed himself the small luxury of a beer at Rolla Dinsdale's Appaloosa Saloon. Unfortunately, the Appaloosa was a favorite retreat of the Verde Flats cattlemen, and Dacey Hargrove was present that night, as proddy as ever and not about to miss a chance to bait a farmhand. Reluctantly, Ezra agreed to fight him.

"In a side alley you say?" drawled Larry.

"'Tween the saloon and the place next door, Gruner's Bakery," said Ezra.

"Big crowd?"

"Well, no. I guess most of Mister Dinsdale's customers had seen it all before. Dacey or his brother beatin' up some Valley man. So there was only a few came out to watch."

"You remember who?"

"Uh huh. There was Burch McNear. He's foreman at Diamond Seven. Couple other cattlemen. Mister Floren that owns the ranch out near the valley, Broken Arrow. And one of his men. I think his name's Nicholls. And that gentleman lawyer, Mister Rossiter? He was there too."

"Who landed the first punch?" demanded Larry.

"Dacey." Ezra grinned ruefully. "Put me right down with that first punch, I'm tellin' you. Well, it was him forced the fight, so I wasn't gonna be the one that started it. I just got back on my feet and, from then on, had to do the best I could."

"So you scored one that downed him for good and all," nodded Larry. "And then what?"

"Burch McNear hollered for the law. When the deputies come to the alley, McNear and the cattlemen were pickin' Dacey up and Mister Rossiter was sayin' how they better take home to Doc Sharman. Mister Floren told the deputies to lock me up because maybe Dacey was hurt bad. Well, they did that, and I been here ever since." Ezra then declared, "I aim to take my chances in court. All I want is a fair trial, you know? I didn't start out to kill

Dacey. If they call it murder . . . "

"I'm bettin' on manslaughter," muttered Larry.

"I'll take my chances," Ezra repeated. "But I got no chance if I'm dragged out and lynched. And, if any valley hands busted me out of here, that'd be near as bad, wouldn't it? I need to say my piece in court."

"Your old man got cash enough for a lawyer?" asked Larry.

"Only lawyer I know about is Mister Rossiter," said Ezra. "But they say he's courtin' Miss Selma Hargrove. Seems like I'll have to do my own talkin'."

"Havin' a lawyer is better," frowned Larry. "Every man to his trade, kid." He matched stares with the prisoner a moment longer, then shook his head and complained, "You're a big disappointment to me."

"Why?" asked the crest fallen Ezra.

"I believe everything you told me," Larry said bitterly. "If I pegged you for a lyin', snivellin' no-account, everything'd be easier for me. I'd tear that tin star off of the beanpole and me and him'd get the hell out of this territory. But now I'm stuck with an unlucky sodbuster that deserves his day in court."

"Oh?" Ezra shrugged uncomfortably. "Well, I sure apologize."

"That's no help," grouched Larry, turning away.

He returned to the office and, to the consternation of Stretch and the jailer, announced his intention of riding to Diamond Seven.

"But — damnitall . . . !" began Stretch.

"Time for somebody to talk turkey to Rand Hargrove," Larry said impatiently. "If we got to fight every hombre in Hargrove's bunkhouse gang, that's just what we'll do. But I ought to try talkin' first. No use swappin' gab with his lynch-happy crew. Better to parley with the boss-man."

"Well, okay," nodded Stretch. "Do you damndest. But take care, ol' buddy."

"Cowhands and farm-boys ready to leap at each other's throats," mumbled Larry, as Cobb opened up for him. "If it ain't cowhands and farm-boys, it's cowhands and miners or cowhands and sheepherders. Just once, why couldn't we find a town where nobody hates nobody?"

He emerged from the law office and descended to his waiting horse. Behind him, he heard the door secured, the key rattling in the lock, the thud of the bar falling into position. Disgruntled, he mounted and rode half-way along the next block. Until he heard the pounding hooves and the wild whoops, it was his intention to accost a local and ask directions to Verde Flats and Diamond Seven. He turned his horse and watched the seven riders raising dust in front of the jailhouse, their horses milling. One, a passably handsome young fellow, blond and burly, brandished a rope. People scattered for cover as he bellowed his challenge.

"You in the office — you with the

tin badge! This is Chuck Hargrove and I'm here to square accounts for my brother!"

A heated retort erupted from the office window and, to Larry's surprise, the voice was not his partner's. Cobb was showing spirit.

"Sheriff don't waste time talkin' to you trouble-makers! All acounts'll be squared at the trial, here?"

"Shuddup, Cobb!" jeered Chuck Hargrove. "I'll do my talkin' to the saddlebum sheriff — if he's got nerve enough to show himself."

Grimacing in exasperation, Larry swung down, tied the sorrel to a post and began moving toward the Diamond Seven men. From the window, having nudged the turnkey aside, Stretch called a command.

"Say your piece, boy. Then vamoose."

"Vamoose be damned!" scowled Chuck. "Now you listen good! There's just no way you can hold out against every cattleman in this territory! That's what you're up against and don't you forget it. All of us. Every hand from every spread. So make it easy on yourself. Send Gregg out. You turn him over to me — right here and now — or . . . !"

"I'm holdin' my prisoner for trial," declared Stretch.

"The hell you are!" countered Chuck. "Send him out or, by Judas, we'll set fire to your jail and you can fry — all three of you!"

"That'd be a fool move, boy," warned Stretch.

"You had your chance!" raged Chuck. He was turning in his saddle, barking orders to his companions, as Larry reached him. "Pike! Curly! Fetch coal-oil! We're gonna burn 'em out!"

What followed was so swift, so decisive, that Chuck Hargrove's buddies were caught with their mouths open. Larry transferred Chuck from his horse to the dust by the simple action of jerking one of his feet from stirrup and heaving. Over the animal's other side Chuck hurtled, going down with a resounding thud. Larry slapped the horse, causing it to prance clear. Then he bent, whisked Chuck's Colt from its holster, hooked his left arm about his neck and hauled him to his feet. He was facing the Diamond Seven men now, but with Chuck his prisoner, the muzzle of the cocked Colt pressed to the blond head.

One of the horsemen was suddenly frantic, gasping a warning.

"That's Chuck's own iron — and it's hair-trigger! Easy, for pity's sake . . . !"

"Chuck's jailbait," Larry said curtly. "But, if any of you heroes makes a wrong move, Chuck'll never make it to the calaboose. He'll be awful dead — awful fast. Now unstrap your sidearms and throw'em in that water trough other side of the street, then hustle on back to Diamond Seven and give your boss a message from the Keever County law. Better not be any burnin', savvy? If this jail burns, Chuck'll burn along with it. Anyway . . . " He shrugged contemptuously. "If I catch any fool totin' coal-oil, I'll make him *drink* it."

He dragged the bug-eyed Chuck to the steps, pausing there, staring hard at the six. One of them took the riderless animal by its rein. They retreated to the other side of Main and, watched by Larry, Stretch, Cobb and a great many townfolk, unbuckled their weapons and dropped them into the trough. They wheeled their mounts to move out and the drag rider could not resist a taunt.

"You just signed your own death-warrant, tall feller."

"I keep doin' that," Larry retorted. "Don't know any better. But I'm still around."

4

Hot Tempers and Cold Nerves

AS Larry hustled his prisoner up to the porch, Stretch opened the office door and, hefting a Colt, cautiously surveyed the immediate vicinity.

"They've backed off — for a while," Larry told him.

He shoved Chuck Hargrove into the office, followed him and lowered the hammer of Chuck's pistol and laid it on the desk.

"Hair-trigger, I heard a feller say," muttered Stretch, watching the street from the doorway.

"By glory, that was somethin' to see!" enthused Cobb. "I'm damn glad I was sober, so I could see how you did it!"

"If you think you're gonna get away

with . . . !" began Chuck.

"Stand real quiet, kid," ordered Cobb. "Stretch, what d'you say? Larry called him jailbait, and I sure go along with that."

"So do I," grinned Stretch. "Runt, what do we call what he did?"

"Incitin' a riot maybe," shrugged Larry. "Disturbin' the peace. Threatenin' the law. You got reason enough for stashin' him in the pokey to cool off."

"You hombres are loco!" breathed Chuck. "The old man ain't gonna hold still for this. Every rider on the Diamond Seven payroll will be comin' in to . . ."

"To do what?" challenged Larry. "Burn the jail — with you inside it? Let me tell you somethin', hotshot. You're a mighty important prisoner. As long as we hold you, I'm bettin' your old man'll leave us be."

"You don't know Rand Hargrove," warned Chuck.

"Not yet," agreed Larry. "But I plan on meetin' him real soon."

101

"You still ridin' out to Diamond Seven?" frowned Cobb.

"After arrestin' Hargrove's boy — and you with no badge?" drawled Stretch. "I don't think Hargrove's gonna like that."

"You're gonna be sorry you crossed Diamond Seven," Chuck predicted with an ugly grin.

"Had to do what I did, hotshot," said Larry. "The beanpole and me, we just don't take kindly to lynch-talk."

"It irks us," said Stretch.

"Move up close to the desk and turn out your pockets," ordered Cobb.

Chuck cursed indignantly, but obeyed. Deftly, Larry moved the hair-trigger sixgun out of his reach, ejecting the shells and letting it dangle from the gunrack by the trigger-guard. He kept a hard eye on rebellious Chuck while Cobb frisked him, emptied the contents of his pockets into a paper sack and locked them in the office safe.

"Look at No-account Newt," jibed Chuck. "The suddenly-sober turnkey.

How long can you keep it up, Newt?"

"Don't fret about me, kid," muttered Cobb, taking up the keyring. "Better to fret about yourself."

To the new prisoner's chagrin, the jailer unlocked the cell directly opposite the one occupied by Ezra Gregg.

"You can't do this!" he raged. "You can't put me where I have to look at the polecat sodbuster that killed my brother!"

He gave Cobb the back of his hand. The blow caused Cobb's face to smart, but he maintained control of himself. Though many years older than the hothead, he was also heftier, more muscular. Had he thrown all his weight behind the punch to Chuck's face, he might have fractured his jaw or broken his nose. At that, the impact drove Chuck clear across the cell to collapse on the bunk. As he secured the cell-door, Cobb reproached him with a certain dignity.

"Sorry you made me do that, kid, and sorry if I hurt you. But, you know, a man my age can't let any young whippersnapper backhand him. Didn't old Rand teach you respect for your elders?"

"Respect . . . ?" groaned Chuck, holding a hand to his left eye. "Respect for the most lowdown drunk in Keever?"

For a moment, Cobb was just a mite self-conscious.

"That's what I used to be," he admitted. "But now I'm temperance again. Remember that — next time you take a swing at me."

Larry had joined Stretch in the street doorway. He was about to move out when Stretch said ruefully, "I wouldn't have thought of it — grabbin' Hargrove's son for insurance. Got to hand it to you, runt. Your brain is smarter'n mine."

"Well," shrugged Larry. "Hargrove already lost one son. Ain't likely he'd take a chance on losin' the other. I don't reckon you'll see firebrands 'tween now and the day they try Ezra."

"Took to Ezra, didn't you?" prodded Stretch. "Listen, wait till you see Libby. She's got the purtiest eyes. Big and brown and . . ."

"Go polish your badge," Larry said in disgust, as he crossed the threshold. "And keep that door locked, consarn you!"

"Just like old times, runt," Stretch called after him. "It purely comforts me, the way you boss me around."

A passer-by offered directions to Verde Flats and, minutes later, Larry was riding north out of Keever at a steady clip, determined to catch up with Chuck Hargrove's six cohorts; it was his intention to keep them in sight while crossing Diamond Seven range.

Late morning, traveling Hargrove land with the homebound six some 150 yards ahead of him, he took time to scan Diamond Seven's vast acreage, the lush green plain whereon the big herds grazed. Yes, big was the word. He guessed Hargrove to be one of a breed he knew well, an old-time cattleman who, from his first breed-herd, had built a Longhorn empire and won a great deal of power and prestige, maybe more than he knew how to handle. Rand Hargrove, he anticipated, would prove to be a replica of every big shot cattle baron with whom he had tangled in his wandering years. And he had tangled with quite a few.

Three Hargrove riders emerged from chaparral a short distance to Larry's left, sighted him and kept coming. He didn't tense up. Their demeanor was friendly enough, one of them waving, another calling a howdy. He kept the sorrel moving steadily toward the distant buildings. They joined him, matching his speed, asking questions. He gave nothing away.

"If you're lookin' to throw in with Diamond Seven, you sure picked the right time," he was told. "Mister Hargrove's hirin'!"

"Needs all the help he can get?" drawled Larry.

"He's just bound to take you

on," predicted the youngest of the three. "Plain enough you're an old hand at workin' cattle." He grinned and winked. "And you pack plenty hardware. Long gun as well as a hogleg. The old man'll sure approve."

"I sure hope so," Larry confided. "Plain truth is I don't crave trouble with Mister Rand Hargrove".

His timing was perfect and his luck holding. Riding in with three of Hargrove's men, he escaped the attention of the group assembled in the yard fronting the big ranch-house. The six disarmed hotheads were reporting another reversal to a grim-faced Rand Hargrove and an incredulous Burch McNear. Hargrove's wife was on the porch, listening. Also listening, keenly interested, was Selma, standing by a handsome surrey to which a pair of matched blacks were harnessed. She had been about to leave for a visit to the county seat and was dressed for the occasion. Deep blue gown and fashionable chapeau. Profoundly impressed by her beauty, Larry had to discipline himself to keep his eyes off her and well and truly on the man he assumed to be the Diamond Seven boss.

He reined up with the cowpokes just as Hargrove turned on his foreman furiously.

"You said you sent Chuck to the north line-shack! Now these men tell me he took 'em to Keever and got himself thrown in jail, damn it . . . !"

"I can't be in two places at one time, Rand," retorted McNear. "How could I know he'd head for town?"

"But for that other stranger, the one that pulled Chuck off of his horse, we might've spooked that saddlebum sheriff," one of the men assured the rancher.

"You forgot somethin', Colby," scowled Hargrove. "It wasn't up to you — or Chuck. *I* give the orders!" He was still eyeing McNear. "Second time, Burch, and that's twice too often. First some saddletramp out-bluffs a dozen

Diamond Seven hands — and now another stranger takes Chuck — with Chuck's own gun! Tell me what the hell's happenin' to this outfit! There was a time no man'd dare stand against us!"

"This hombre moved so slick, Mister Hargrove," another waddy complained. "He was right there — haulin' Chuck off of his horse before we could . . . " His gaze had strayed and now, incredulously, he gaped at the brawny outsider on the sorrel, loosed a gasp and pointed. "Hey! That's *him*! That's the jasper that did it!"

All eyes turned to Larry. The men with whom he had ridden in warily nudged their mounts clear and, unflinchingly, he met Hargrove's baleful glare. McNear, first to find his voice, declared, "He's got to be loco, comin' right here to Diamond Seven — after what he did."

"To me, he don't look loco," muttered Hargrove. "Just proddy."

"What're you waitin' for?" McNear

109

challenged the ranch-hands. "Get him off that horse — and don't do it gentle!"

"I'll do my talkin' from here," countered Larry, his cold gaze switching to the foreman. "You're the ramrod? All right, mister, somethin' you better understand. Anybody crowds me, I'll defend myself. Any fool pulls a gun . . ."

"There'll be no gunplay here," Hargrove said sternly.

"Won't be me starts it," shrugged Larry. He then doffed his Stetson to Selma and to her mother. "Ladies, my apologies. Like you to know I came here to talk, not to fight."

"Is my son hurt?" demanded Sophie.

"Looked plenty spry when the turn-key marched him into the jailhouse, ma'am," drawled Larry. "Too bad I had to shove him off his horse, but it could've been worse. It was only his pride got hurt."

"By thunder, you're a nervy sonofagun," growled Hargrove. "I don't know how you can face me."

"I should be ashamed?" challenged Larry. "Your boy was makin' lynch-talk, Mister Hargrove, claimin' he'd burn the jail. Maybe that sets right with you, but it don't set right with me. And that's why I can face you."

"Rand, you don't have to take this kind of back-talk from no saddlebum," McNear said grimly.

"So far, this man has said nothing unreasonable," remarked Selma.

"You keep out of this," chided Hargrove. "As for you . . ." He stared hard at Larry, "You got the look of a cattleman sure enough, and it sticks in my craw — a man like you — sidin' with sodbusters, helpin' protect the farm-hand who killed my son."

"We ain't takin' sides, the sheriff or me," retorted Larry. "Wouldn't care a bent cent if Ezra Gregg was a prospector, a cardsharp or a sheepherder. Whatever kind of man he is, he rates fair trial. That's how it ought to be for every man."

"Who the hell are you anyway?"

demanded Hargrove.

"Name of Valentine," offered Larry.

"You and that saddletramp sheriff . . . " began Hargrove.

"Partners from way back," said Larry.

"You wear no badge," Hargrove observed.

"Didn't figure I'd need one," shrugged Larry. "Man talks good sense, he don't need to back it up with a six-pointed star. Not if what he says is true."

"I'll give you a few minutes," decided Hargrove, "but only because you're holdin' Chuck hostage."

"Hostage nothin'," growled Larry. "He's locked up for his own protection, not ours. On the loose and proddy, he'd buy more trouble than you could pull him out of." He gestured to the six unarmed waddies. "He planned on burnin' the jail. If you don't believe me, ask *them*."

"They already told me," said Hargrove. "And I sure wouldn't have blamed Chuck if he'd done it."

"You don't realize what you're saying, Rand!" protested his wife. "You couldn't condone such a terrible thing!"

"Dacey's dead and the Gregg boy killed him!" gasped Hargrove.

"Accidentally," insisted Selma.

For a moment, Larry feared he would have to move between father and daughter; Hargrove appeared ready to turn on her. When he spoke again, his voice was husky. Plainly he was controlling himself with difficulty.

"Said I'd give you a few minutes. Burch, get rid of these men This is a family matter. But you can stay."

The hired hands drifted away toward a bunkhouse. Neither Hargrove nor his foreman had invited Larry to dismount, so he hooked a leg about his saddlehorn, content to stay on the sorrel while talking turkey. Producing his makings, he eyed the woman politely.

"By your leave, ladies."

Selma was impassive, but her mother

nodded gently and remarked, "It's a long time since I was asked permission by a man who wished to smoke."

"Whatever you have to say, Valentine, say it fast," ordered Hargrove.

"Yeah, sure," nodded Larry. While talking, he rolled a cigarette one-handed, scratched a match on his thumbnail and lit up. "It could be Dacey still alive and Ezra in a grave — you ever stop to think of that? Could've been Ezra's head hit the wall, and how'd you feel if Marvin Gregg hollered murder and vowed he'd lynch your son? You don't have to answer that question. Just think about it."

"You got your nerve," growled McNear, "talkin' this way to a man as important as Rand Hargrove."

"McNear's your name, right?" prodded Larry. "Well, I'll tell you, McNear, you ain't the kind of hombre I can respect."

"Now listen, you . . . !" began McNear.

"Instead of tryin' to break it up,

you stood by and watched those young bucks tradin' punches," accused Larry.

"No man ever put Dacey down!" blustered McNear.

"Has to be a first time for everything," Larry said bitterly. "And don't forget . . . " He looked at Hargrove again, "Ezra didn't start that fight. Dacey forced him into it — and there were plenty in the saloon who'll bear witness to that."

"Not if they want to stay healthy!" retorted Hargrove.

He said it impulsively and at once regretted it, though he went right on glaring at Larry.

"You own the circuit-judge?" Larry quietly challenged. "You throw so big a shadow in this territory, you could threaten witnesses and get away with it?"

"I'll discuss that point with Arnold," decided Selma. "He's taking me to lunch today."

"Not one word of support do I hear from you, girl!" raged Hargrove.

"Buyin' you a high-class education was my worst mistake. It made you a know-it-all and turned you against me!"

"Rand, you have no right to say that," frowned his wife.

"Your only mistake was in not doing the same for your sons," Selma told her father. "If they were as educated as I, they'd have known better than to behave as they did. Dacey's arrogance was the death of him. And now Chuck's in jail — so I hope you're satisfied."

She nodded to her mother, climbed to the surrey seat and gathered the reins. As the vehicle rolled out of the yard, Larry cursed under his breath, regretting this heated exchange between the rancher and his imperious daughter, resenting it too. It seemed unlikely Hargrove would listen to reason in his present mood, but he had come here to appeal for reason and had to make the attempt.

"No use blamin' the farmers if this mess builds up to a shootin' war," he warned. "It'll be on your shoulders."

116

"You tell that saddletramp sheriff there'll be no escape for Dacey's killer — specially in court!" raged Hargrove. "No lawyer of this county would risk my anger by agreein' to defend that killer!"

"If that's a fact, Ezra won't be tried next time Judge Mayo comes to Keever," said Larry. "I don't believe any judge'd let some farmboy conduct his own defense. So Ezra'd be held over. They'd have to postpone the trial and send for a lawyer from outside the county to defend him. And that'll take time."

Hargrove's face was pallid.

"You got more nerve than sense," he breathed. "One of my sons is dead and you put the other in jail and I got a hired hand laid up in the bunkhouse with his good arm bullet-busted. Diamond Seven's an unhealthy place for you to visit, Valentine, but you came anyway. So maybe Burch is right about you. You're as loco as he claims."

"Had to say my piece," shrugged Larry. "Now I've said it and I figure, if you're smart enough to build so fine a spread, you'll maybe think on what I've said."

"Your time's up," Hargrove said curtly. "Get off my land."

Larry nodded resignedly as he eased his boot around his saddlehorn and down to stirrup. He doffed his hat to Sophie Hargrove while wheeling the sorrel. And then, without a backward glance, he began retracing his route across Diamond Seven range.

Later, riding the town trail, he recognized the surrey stalled directly ahead. The blond beauty accorded him a smile when he reined up.

"Why not tie your horse behind and travel with me?" she invited. "Unless, of course, curious women bother you. Believe me, Mister Valentine, I *am* curious."

"Lady, if your pa got to hear of it . . . " he began.

"Are you afraid of my father?"

118

she challenged. He shook his head. "Neither am I — as you may have noticed. Well?"

"Well," he shrugged. "I got a question for you anyway."

"Wonderful!" Her eyes danced. "I've aroused the interest of a confirmed bachelor."

He dismounted, eyeing her perplexedly. "How'd you know I'm a bachelor? Why couldn't I be ten-fifteen years wed, and daddy to a half-dozen kids?"

She chuckled good-humoredly while he tied the sorrel behind the vehicle. Not until he was sharing the seat with her did she assure him, "Some bachelors, the rentless kind, are easily identified." She flicked the blacks and they moved again. "You, Mister Valentine, are hardly the pipe-puffing, settled-down type, the kind who takes his ease in a rocking chair in the late afternoon and contentedly surveys all he has achieved, be it a grazing herd or a crop ready for harvesting."

"All right," he shrugged. "So you're

high-educated and smart at sizin' people up."

"Does that bother you?" she asked.

"Not one little bit," he drawled. "Woman's got a right to use her brain the best way she knows how."

"I wish my father felt that way," said Selma. "You must have noticed . . . "

"I noticed," he nodded.

"You said you have a question for me," she reminded him.

"You said you're curious," he recalled. "Ladies first."

"My questions can wait," she said. "What did you want to ask me?"

"You got a lawyer-friend," said Larry. "If he's courtin' you, it figures he can't be hired to defend young Ezra at his trial. But maybe he knows another lawyer hereabouts?"

"You intend arranging for a defense counsel?"

"Somebody ought to think of it."

"You won't need to ask my friend Arnold Rossiter. I can name the other lawyers of Keever County, one still practicing, the other retired. Floyd Clemenshaw is a brilliant attorney, but he wouldn't be available."

"Any special reason?"

"An excellent reason, Mister Valentine. He's county prosecutor."

"That leaves the old feller who quit the business," frowned Larry.

"Leon Peach is no older than Arnold," she smiled. "In his early thirties I believe. I'm afraid he chose the wrong profession."

"Couldn't make it as a lawyer?" prodded Larry.

"Certainly not in Keever County," said Selma. "He hung out his shingle and I'm sure he did his best, but his best just wasn't good enough. A sad record, Mister Valentine. Every case he fought, Floyd Clemenshaw made a fool of him. He became discouraged and, with two children to raise, had to find other means of supporting his family." She chuckled softly. "He is now a barber, believe it or not. Has a little place on Sabina Road, single-storied

121

with living quarters behind the shop."

"You don't much admire a man who fails," Larry accused.

"Don't jump to conclusions," she chided. "I'm truly sorry for that little man. I've met his wife a few times and . . ."

"And sized her up," he guessed.

"I think poor Mister Peach is well and truly under her thumb," she confided. "Constance Peach is a somewhat over-bearing woman, very forceful."

"No man, wed or single, should let a woman boss him around," grouched Larry.

"Will you answer my questions now?" she begged. "I'm trying to understand how two strangers, men never seen in Keever before, could make such an impression in so short a time. As I hear it, the man called Henderson . . ."

"Emerson," corrected Larry.

" . . . challenged a dozen Diamond Seven men, intimidated them and was appointed to replace Sheriff Pooley — all within an hour of arriving in Keever."

"Uh huh. That's about the size of it."

"And, almost as quickly, you've become identified as his supporter."

"We've been helpin' each other a long time, Miss Selma. Been partners since the war."

"Let's dispense with formality," she urged. "Call me Selma if you wish."

"Sure," he shrugged. "And I'm Larry to my friends."

I've no intention of becoming your enemy," she smiled. "So Larry it is. And now will you explain?"

"You mean — what's in it for us?" challenged Larry.

"Yes, what exactly?" she demanded. "Excitement? Antagonism toward wealthy cattlemen? An urge to make a name for yourselves?"

"For a high-educated lady, you sure guess wild," he muttered. "This kind of excitement we'd as soon pass up.

We can handle it, but that don't mean we crave it. We got nothin' against big-shots like your old man, so long as they don't get to thinkin' they're bigger'n the law. And makin' a name for ourselves? Listen, a reputation is nothin' but trouble for the likes of us. All we ever wanted was to ramble anyplace we please and mind our own business."

"I find it hard to believe you're aimless," she protested. "Every man is searching for something. Why should you be an exception?"

"Oh, we've been lookin' for somethin' many a long year," he moodily confided. "I don't reckon we'll ever find it, but we keep right on lookin'. And hopin'."

"For . . . ?" she asked.

"Some quiet place," he told her. "Friendly folks with no troubles, nobody tryin' to prove anything, just everybody livin' peaceable with his neighbor."

"You're talking about Utopia, and there's no such place," she warned.

"It's a myth, Larry."

"Maybe," he conceded. "But, like you said, every man searches for somethin'."

"You're not thinking of your Utopia now," she surmised. "Your only concern is Ezra Gregg's problem."

"And *his* only problem," Larry pointed out, "is stayin' alive so he gets his day in court. Poor sonofagun's entitled to that much, right? It was your brother got killed and I'm sorry, but that don't mean Ezra did it deliberate."

She nodded thoughtfully, her gaze on the trail ahead and the handsome blacks. The terrain to either side was pleasing to the eye; this was as picturesque a piece of Nevada as Larry had ever traveled, but he was oblivious to the scenery, as oblivious as his pensive companion.

"I hid my grief — quite skilfully I believe," she mused. "I really do miss Dacey. I mourn him and remember our childhood, the way things were.

A woman should be grateful for a childhood spent as both a kid sister and a big sister. Dacey was the eldest, you see."

"And Chuck the last-born," he nodded.

"I don't really believe Ezra Gregg meant to kill Dacey," she assured him. "And I keep saying that — much to my father's resentment."

"That makes two of us don't believe Ezra's a killer," said Larry. Make that three. I talked to him, and I'm tellin' you Ezra is one mighty puzzled hombre."

"Puzzled?"

"Can't savvy why Dacey died from that bump on his head. Claims Dacey didn't hit that wall hard enough to be killed. Hard enough to get knocked out, sure, but not all *that* hard."

"Don't forget the witnesses," she cautioned. "Arnold was one of them, did you know?"

"So I hear," said Larry. "And I still have to figure a way of makin' things look better for the kid, so I guess I'll have to talk to the doc."

"Very short-sighted nowadays, dear old Doc Sharman," she remarked. "Mayor Keele is quite progressive, but I fear he needs to be reminded of Myron Sharman's age. With the population increasing, this territory needs another physician. Why, there'd be work for two more doctors. And then Myron Sharman could retire at last. Heaven knows he's earned his rest." She eyed him sidelong. "What could the doctor tell you that would help Ezra's case?"

"I don't know," shrugged Larry. "But there has to be somethin'. All I've got to start with is what Ezra said." He pondered the problem a moment, then voiced a hunch. "Suppose, for instance the doc fed Dacey some kind of medicine — the wrong kind. You said he don't see so good any more."

"Almost blind without his spectacles," frowned Selma. "But aren't you clutching at straws?"

"There'll be somethin'," he opined.

"There has to be."

Main Street appeared orderly when they arrived, no shouting mob in the vicinity of the county jail, no more townfolk on the sidewalks as was customary, and most of them pausing to stare at this odd couple, the beautiful daughter of the all-powerful Rand Hargrove and a rough-hewn stranger who had challenged that power. Outside Arnold Rossiter's office they separated, Selma entering the building to be greeted by her most persistent suitor, Larry untying his sorrel and leading it to the law office hitch-rail.

He called to Stretch and the jailer, watching from the front window.

"I'll get back to you in a little while. Gonna visit Doc Sharman."

"Ain't feelin' poorly, are you?" Cobb asked anxiously.

"Just curious," said Larry.

"Newt's fixin' lunch," offered Stretch. "Come and eat when you're through with the doc."

From the law office to the Sharman home, Larry dawdled. By coincidence, he was directed to the doctor's house by the same deadbeat he had encountered before, Ike Jeffers of the diffident demeanor and bloodshot eyes. Absent-mindedly, pre-occupied with his secret thoughts, he pressed a quarter into Jeffers' grimy paw. For this, the barfly would remember him.

He was admitted to the neat house by tiny Adela Sharman, the medico's spouse. She stood only 4 feet 10 inches and was grey-haired, but he assumed she was several years her husband's junior, her movements being brisk and assured, her eyes clear and her speech as yet unmuffled by age. Myron Sharman had been called for an hour ago and taken out to the Flying W ranch to attend an emergency.

"I do hope it's not too bad," she remarked. "The cook tore a hand on a rusty nail, and that can be very serious you know."

"Blood poison," nodded Larry.

"If the wound is treated in time . . . "

"Sure, ma'am. So — uh — better I come by later?"

"If you need medical attention," she said with a bright smile. "Though — good heavens — you look so healthy, so strong!"

"Thank you, ma'am, I'm feelin' fine," he told her. "I only wanted to talk to the doc — about the way Dacey Hargrove died."

"Whatever you wish to know, I'm sure I can tell you as much as Myron," she offered.

"Oh?" He raised an eyebrow. "You were there when Dacey died?"

"Not exactly," she said. "As I recall, neither of us was actually in the surgery at the moment he died. Myron couldn't remember where he'd left his spectacles. He's always doing that, I'm afraid. And, when he left the surgery to look for them, I followed him. Poor Myron, he might have accidentally knocked them from a table and stepped on them. That man makes me so *nervous* when

130

he's hunting around for his spectacles."
She crooked a finger and withdrew
along the hall. "Do you mind if
we talk in the kitchen? I have to
keep his lunch warm, don't want it
to spoil."

For almost a quarter-hour, Larry
sat in the Sharman kitchen with an
attentive ear cocked to little Adela's
recollections of the night of Dacey
Hargrove's death. He interjected a
question or two, but mostly he listened.
She had an eye for detail and a reliable
memory.

Was he any closer to resolving
the crisis confronting Keever County,
any closer to a solution to Ezra's
predicament? He asked himself these
questions after thanking the doctor's
wife and leaving the house.

"Maybe," was his only answer at
this time. "It's just a maybe, but it's
somethin'. At least it's a start."

In the law office, with his partner
about to tote laden plates into the
cellblock, he decided to postpone

131

airing his hunches until partaking of the meal prepared by the turnkey. Chuck Hargrove was mumbling abuse at the other prisoner, until the new sheriff appeared.

5

Visitors Day

STRETCH slid the plates under the cell-doors and warily studied the prisoners, Ezra so quiet, so serious, Chuck sporting a black eye and as arrogant, as rebellious as ever.

"I can hear through that dealwood door," he told Chuck. "How much longer you gonna take it out on Ezra? You think cussin' him is gonna bring your brother back?"

"This killer'll eat hearty now," Chuck grimly predicted. "Dacey bein' dead don't mean nothin' to him."

"You eat hearty too, boy," urged Stretch, as he turned away. "You won't relish your grub. It's likely not as fancy as you eat at Diamond Seven, but you better get used to it, on account of it's the best you'll get till

I'm ready to turn you loose."

Slump-shouldered, Ezra collected his lunch and squatted on his bunk to eat. The connecting door thudded shut behind Stretch. He tried a mouthful, then glanced across at the sandy-haired feller who, since rallying from the blow inflicted by Cobb, had denounced, abused and insulted him, also his family and the whole farming community of Council Valley. Through it all, he had kept his mouth shut, reasoning there was nought to be gained by trying to placate the sorehead in his present condition. He tried it, but not until Chuck's plate was half-empty.

"You — uh — mind if I ask you somethin'?"

"Like what?" Chuck sourly challenged.

"I was just wonderin' . . . " Ezra shrugged and forked up another mouthful. "Wonderin' if it ever happened to you."

"If what happened?" scowled Chuck. "What're you talkin' about?"

"Any feller ever force you into fightin'

134

him?" asked Ezra. "I mean keep after you with the mean-mouthin' and the cussin' till, if you call yourself any kind of man, you just *had* to say you'd fight?"

"I'm a Hargrove," bragged Chuck. "No man tries that on a Hargrove."

"That ain't what I mean." Ezra munched and swallowed and shrugged helplessly. "Well, what's the use me tryin' to explain? Forget it. Pardon me for mentionin' it."

Chuck finished his meal in silence. He fumbled at his empty pockets for tobacco, grimaced irritably. More silence, but only for another minute. That was as long as he could resist asking, "Explain what?"

"You mean what shocked me most?"

"Yeah. That."

Ezra set his plate aside and rose to his feet.

"Take a good look at me," he invited. "Am I bigger'n Dacey was? Taller? Heftier? Stronger?"

"Compared to Dacey . . . " Chuck

grinned contemptuously, "you're puny."

"So how come my punch killed him?" wondered Ezra. "Oh, sure. He fell against the wall, but not all that hard. So I still don't savvy how it could happen that way." He sat down again. "Can *you* savvy it?"

The question won a jeering comment.

"If that's how you aim to defend yourself," grinned Chuck. "if that's the kind of hogwash you plan on feedin' to a judge and jury, I should fret about lynchin' you? Hell! You'll hang yourself with that story. It's weak, sodbuster. It wouldn't buy you time, wouldn't convince *anybody*!"

"I sure hope they'll believe me," frowned Ezra. "It's all I've got."

Chuck laughed derisively and sprawled on his bunk, hands clasped behind his head, eyes on the fly-specked ceiling. Then, after a long moment, he turned his head to covertly study the other prisoner.

Larry, meanwhile, had finished eating and was starting on his first cup of coffee, perching on the stool by the window, pensively studying the street. Stretch ate at the desk, Cobb on the couch, both of them eyeing Larry expectantly. He had recounted details of his confrontation with the Diamond Seven boss, but had not yet confided the reason for his visit to the Sharman home. Now, abruptly, he resumed talking.

"The doc's wife told me how it was that night."

"Meanin' the night young Hargrove was killed?" frowned Cobb.

"Yeah, that night." Larry turned to look him over and to remark to his partner, "He ain't like he was."

"Well, no," agreed Stretch.

"What happened to him?" demanded Larry.

"He quit drinkin'," shrugged Stretch.

"I don't need it any more," Cobb earnestly assured them. "Listen, I'll prove I can forget Beulah." He reached into a hip pocket. "Ever since she ran off with that tinhorn, I've been carryin'

137

a picture of her and longin' for her. But now I'm gonna tear it to pieces — right before your eyes!"

"Hold it," ordered Larry.

"What d'you mean — hold it?" challenged Cobb.

"I mean, before you tear up the picture, we might's well see it," said Larry.

Cobb trudged from the couch to the desk and offered the photograph. Stretch looked at it, winced and said, "Show Larry."

Larry, after studying the picture a moment, frowned incredulously at the turnkey.

"I'm sure sorry for you," said Larry. "But sorrier for the tinhorn." He returned the picture and gestured impatiently. "Tear it up and forget her."

The photograph of Cobb's lost love was torn to shreds and the shreds tossed into the stove, after which Larry talked of his conversation with Adela Sharman.

It seemed circumstances had conspired to relieve Myron Sharman of the chore of examining the befuddled Dace Hargrove. Adela was of the opinion the patient was about to revive when carried into the surgery by Jerry Floren and his hired hand. Also in attendance were lawyer Arnold Rossiter and Burch McNear, the Diamond Seven foreman. Less than efficient without his spectacles, old Myron had hurried from the surgery to look for them.

"And his wife went after him," said Larry. "They found his eye-glasses in the parlor and went on back to the surgery. The lawyer was hustlin' him, sayin' Dacey looked real bad and he better do somethin' for him muy pronto. The doc checked, couldn't find a heartbeat, no pulse."

"Cashed in while the doc was elsewhere, huh?" frowned Stretch.

"Doc and his wife," nodded Larry. "She claims they were gone only a couple minutes. But, when they reached

139

the surgery again, it was all over."

"So there was nothin' Doc could do," Cobb supposed, "except make out a death certificate."

"Cause of death — his heart just quit beatin'," said Larry. "The little lady said, if her man has to testify at the trial, he won't swear it was the head-wound killed Dacey. That's what he told them four jaspers, and you can bet McNear told Dacey's father."

"Yeah, sure," sighed Cobb. "But Rand Hargrove's angry and grievin'. Only thing he wants to remember is Dacey never woke up from bein' clobbered by a farm-boy." He shook his head sadly. "Maybe you got to old Rand today, but I wouldn't count on it."

"You think he'll mount a raid on Council Valley?" asked Stretch.

"What surprises me is it ain't happened already," said Cobb.

"We got somethin' else goin' for us," opined Larry. "Selma and her mother. They don't want a bloody war between cattlemen and farm folks, and that's what they keep tellin' Hargrove. Sooner or later, he's gonna have to heed 'em." He began rolling a cigarette. "Newt, how much d'you know about them four jaspers, McNear, Floren and his hired hand, the lawyer?"

"Don't know any of 'em close," shrugged Cobb. "McNear's been old Rand's foreman for as long as anybody can remember. Jerry Floren runs the Broken Arrow outfit southeast of here. He's the only county cattleman with a spread that close to Council Valley . . ."

"How close?" demanded Larry.

"Maybe a quarter-mile," said Cobb. "Mind now, I never heard of him tanglin' with any sodbusters."

"The other Broken Arrow man, Ezra thinks his name is Nicholls," said Larry.

"That'd be Rudy Nicholls," offered Cobb. "It ain't what you'd call a big outfit, Broken Arrow. There's just Floren and Nicholls and two other fellers, Waincott and Prentice. I don't know 'em personal. Only know their names."

"And the fourth man, Rossiter, he's a right respectable lawyer," mused Larry.

"I never had no dealin's with Mister Rossiter nor any other lawyer," said Cobb. "But I hear talk, hear he's plenty smart, smarter even than the county prosecutor, Floyd Clemenshaw."

"So what d'you think, runt?" prodded Stretch. "You gettin' anywhere?"

"I got damn near nothin'," Larry sourly complained. "Doc Sharman's evidence'll likely help Ezra some. I'm still bettin' on manslaughter. They ought to call it an accident, but they'll likely make it a manslaughter charge . . ."

"Might be the judge'll give Ezra a break," suggested Stretch. "Light sentence?"

"That'll be fine for Ezra," growled Larry. "But only if he's alive to stand trial."

"Mayor Keele claims we could hold off a whole damn army from right where we're settin'," said Stretch. "And I reckon I agree with him. We got guns and plenty ammunition, enough grub to last a couple weeks if we have to hold out that long. I'm tellin' you, runt, we could fort up and raise hell with any bunch tries rushin' us."

"We could do that," nodded Larry.

"All three of us," stressed Cobb. "I'm paid by the county and, by damn, them councilmen're gonna get their money's worth. Drunk, I couldn't hit the barn wall. But — the way I am now — I can shoot straight enough to . . ."

"That's what you want?" challenged Larry. He frowned from Cobb to Stretch. "You too?"

"You know me, runt," Stretch said self-consciously. "Only time I fight is when there's no other way."

"Stay on your toes and keep your eyes peeled, sure," urged Larry. "But don't go haywire like them Diamond Seven hotheads, don't open up on any cowhand ridin' by."

"I don't aim to," Stretch assured him.

Some 45 minutes later, when Larry was rising to move out in search of a Lawyer-turned-barber, he chanced to glance out the window. Followed by the admiring eyes of every male in sight, Selma Hargrove was crossing from the opposite sidewalk.

"Company comin'," he announced. "Mind your manners, stringbean. Get ready to meet Chuck's sister."

"He can have a visitor?" Cobb asked Stretch.

"Where's the harm?" shrugged Stretch. "If any of Ezra's kin came by, I'd let 'em see him. Same with the Hargroves."

As the blonde woman climbed to the porch, Cobb raised the bar, unlocked and opened the street-door and accorded her a respectful nod.

"Afternoon, Miss Selma."

She advanced to the threshold, flashed Larry an amiable smile and, with keen interest, studied the taller

144

Texan rising to greet her.

"So this is your friend, Sheriff Emerson."

"You can call him Stretch," offered Larry.

"My pleasure, Miss Selma," mumbled Stretch.

"He's shy," she observed. "But not when facing a dozen of my father's most unruly men."

"If you're here to visit with your brother, you're plumb welcome," Stretch assured her.

"Thank you," she murmured. "I carry no weapon, concealed or otherwise, I give you my word."

"Good enough for me, Miss Selma," said Stretch.

"I won't stay long," she promised, as Cobb opened the cell-block door. "May I leave this with Chuck?" She exhibited a paper sack. "Just some tobacco and a few items I bought at Bartholomew's — handerkerchiefs — a shirt. It seemed easier than traveling back to the ranch."

"I don't mind at all," said Stretch. "Newt, let the lady into the cell if she wants."

When the county's most beautiful citizen appeared, her brother grimaced irritably. The other prisoner got to his feet, uncomfortable, ill at ease but determined not to avoid her eyes. She turned to look at him while Cobb unlocked the cell where her brother waited. He nodded wistfully and addressed her.

"Yes, ma'am, I'm Ezra Gregg. And I ain't ashamed . . . "

"You got no right to talk to Selma!" scowled Chuck.

"I ain't ashamed my pa's a farmer," said Ezra. "I'm sorry for your grief and sorry Dacey's dead. 'Scuse me. That's all I wanted to say."

"Thank you," she said softly. "And I am sorry for *you*, Ezra Gregg. I've never believed you meant to kill Dacey."

"I didn't, and that's gospel truth," he earnestly assured her. "Ready, Miss Selma?" asked Cobb.

She nodded. He swung the door open, waited for her to enter, then resecured it and returned to the office. She sat beside her brother on the bunk, ruefully inspected his black eye and offered the comforts purchased at the general store.

"Just some things you'll be needing."

"You oughtn't have come, sis," he growled. "Thanks, but you didn't have to do this."

"I was in town anyway, having lunch with Arnold," she told him. "And Mother was distressed to hear of your arrest. At least I'll be able to assure her you're safe and well. I won't mention your black eye."

In the office, Larry was thoughfully studying the wall-map to the right of the cellblock entrance, noting the location of strategically important areas, Verde Flats to the northest, Council Valley far to the southeast. Stretch, about to build a smoke, flinched and spilled tobacco. Cobb was calling to him worriedly from his position at the window. Cocking an ear to the thud of hooves, Stretch asked, "How many of 'em? How many ornery cowpokes this time?"

"You're hearin' team-horses," muttered the turnkey. "Oh, hell. They sure picked a helluva time for a visit."

"Who?" demanded Larry.

"Gregg wagon's stallin' out front," said Cobb. "Looks like the kid's folks're gonna meet a couple Hargroves." He frowned at the Texans. "Can we let that happen? It'll be — uh — kind of a nervous situation."

"What d'you say, runt?" asked Stretch.

"Why ask me?" shrugged Larry. "You're the sheriff."

"Aw, c'mon, damnitall . . . !" pleaded Stretch.

"You want Libby to see a spooked sheriff through them big brown eyes of hers?" taunted Larry. "Get a hold of yourself, big feller."

"Well — what am I gonna *do*?" fretted Stretch.

"If any of Ezra's kin came by, you

said . . . " Larry reminded him.

"All right," sighed Stretch. "All right."

"You took time to size up Libby," drawled Larry. "I'm more interested in Marve Gregg — so *I'll size him* up."

"Okay, Stretch?" prodded Cobb.

"Let 'em in," said Stretch.

Marvin Gregg, burly, blunt-featured and grey-thatched, was garbed in his Sunday-best, a grey broadcloth suit that had seen better days. On the porch, he stood between his plump and apprehensive wife and his slender, eager-eyed daughter. Nora and Libby Gregg wore their best gowns and poke bonnets. Cobb opened up for them and motioned them to enter. Larry turned from the wall-map, bared his head and surveyed them impassively. Libby, he noted, had eyes only for the acutely embarrassed Stretch.

"Sheriff Emerson, Ma and Pa'd take it kindly if you'd allow us to visit with Ezra," she murmured.

"Mister Gregg — ma'am — right

proud to meet you," mumbled Stretch.

"Likewise," grunted the farmer. He appraised both Texans. "Libby was plenty excited. I though maybe she had it wrong. Told me the new sheriff was rigged like a ranch-hand."

"This here's my partner, Larry Valentine," offered Stretch. "Miss Libby didn't make no mistake, Mister Gregg. We was born and raised in Texas cow country."

"And we don't hold with lynchin'," Larry said gently. "That's why my nervous buddy is wearin' that star, Mister Gregg. It's just temporary, you understand. But, for as long as he wears that star, your boys's gonna stay healthy — healthy enough to stand up in court and face a judge and jury."

"My Ezra . . . ?" began Nora.

"He's fine, ma'am," muttered Cobb. "Real steady."

"I'm here to see my son," frowned Gregg, "and to give my word there'll be no Council Valley men tryin' to bust Ezra out of this jail. What he did he'll answer for. That's what he wants — and what I want too." He spread his arms. "Newt Cobb, do your duty."

"Howzat again?" blinked Cobb.

"Try searchin' Nora or the girl and I'll break your arm," said Gregg. "But you're entitled to search me. You only got my word I won't try to give Ezra a pistol, a knife, a hacksaw . . ."

"Now, Marvin, that's plain foolish," chided his wife.

"Pa's joshin'," Libby said apologetically.

"Dead serious," insisted Gregg.

"Sheriff's only got your word, like you say," muttered Larry. "But your word's good enough for him." He glanced at Stretch. "Right?"

"Right," nodded Stretch. "Won't be no search, Mister Gregg. But, before Newt takes you folks in there, you better know I'm holdin' another prisoner, and that other prisoner's got a visitor."

"Chuck Hargrove was actin' too ornery for his own good," explained Cobb.

"You got — Dacey Hargrove's brother in this jail?" Gregg asked incredulously.

"His sister's with him right now," said Larry. "You folks ever meet her?"

"A time or two," sighed Nora. "At church Sundays."

"You don't have to wait, ma'am," offered Stretch. "If you want to see Ezra rightaway, that's fine by me."

"No reason we should wait, I guess," reflected Gregg.

"This way, folks," said Stretch. The Greggs moved past him after he opened the cellblock entrance. Larry joined him and, together, they watched the farmer and his womenfolk move slowly along the passage and pause by Ezra's cell. After trading greetings with Ezra, they turned to look into the cell opposite. Gregg removed his hat. Libby and her mother nodded politely.

Over his shoulder, Larry muttered a command to Cobb.

"Fetch chairs."

Cobb made short work of toting

chairs into the cellblock, positioning them in front of Ezra's cell-door. When he returned to the office, Larry jerked a thumb.

"Keep watchin' the street."

"Damn right," grunted Cobb, moving to the window again.

The Texans listened intently to the farmer's short speech.

"Miss Selma, us Greggs're mighty sorry your brother died from fightin' our Ezra. You'll oblige me by tellin' your parents how we feel about it."

"Thank you, Mister Gregg," murmured Selma. "You may be sure I'll convey your sentiments to Mother and Dad."

"Have to ask you to pardon our backs now," said Gregg, helping his wife seat herself, "while we visit with our boy."

"You hear that?" Stretch whispered. "That sodbuster — by golly — he's got dignity."

"More of it than Rand Hargrove," muttered Larry.

While Ezra conversed quietly with his

parents and sister, Chuck reproached Selma softly, but bitterly.

"If Pa heard you talkin' so polite with them Greggs, it'd break his heart."

"I doubt that," said Selma. "And how did it sound to *you*, Chuck? Was it so disloyal, my speaking to Mister Gregg as courteously as he spoke to me?"

"You're gettin' me all mixed up," he complained.

"Won't you try to learn from what you've just seen?" she begged. "Chuck, this is how intelligent, civilized people behave in time of grief and stress. The Greggs are simple folk, but decent. Isn't that obvious to you?"

"Dacey's dead and . . ."

"And Ezra didn't mean for him to die, didn't plan his death."

"But . . ."

"*Think*, Chuck." She took his hand in hers and held it tight. "While ever you have to stay here, you'll have time to think — reasonably. Ponder the whole terrible tragedy with an open

154

mind. Ask yourself — does Ezra Gregg really deserve to be called a killer?" Abruptly, she released his hand and rose to her feet. "I should leave now, give the Greggs a chance to speak more freely to their son."

As she moved to the cell-door, Stretch hustled along to open up for her. She thanked him with a smile, stepped into the passage and, while he closed and relocked the door, nodded reassuringly to Ezra. Noting that, Chuck gritted his teeth. Escorted back to the office by the taller Texan, she thanked them for their attention. Cobb raised the bar on the street-door, opened it and let her out.

"Some lady, huh?" he remarked, when she was out of earshot.

"Real quality," nodded Stretch. "Uh — runt — how d'you like Libby?"

"Cute little sprig," shrugged Larry. "But I wouldn't get any ideas if I was you. She's too young for you."

"Well . . ." frowned Stretch.

"And she deserves better," opined Larry.

"Thanks a heap," grouched Stretch. "Any other hombre said that, I'd bust his jaw."

"When her time comes, she ought to have a steady man," Larry said mercilessly. "The kind of husband who'll hanker to hang around the house when his day's chores are done, sit by the fire with her, watch her sewin' baby clothes. And he won't get restless, won't be all the time cravin' to saddle up and get to driftin'. You think you can be that kind of man? Your decision, ol' buddy. You ain't tied to me, and I sure won't stand in your way."

"For a gal so special, a man could change," declared Stretch.

"*Some* men could change their ways," countered Larry. "Some never could. For some, it'd be too late. It's up to you. Me, I ain't gonna talk of it no more."

Chuck Hargrove lay on his bunk, puffed on a cigarette and moodily stared at the ceiling. He wasn't trying to eavesdrop. It would have been futile anyway; the Greggs had plenty to say to their son, but were saying it quietly. After a moment, a tingling of his neck-hairs warned him he was under observation. He turned his head and, to his disquiet, saw Libby at his cell-door, peering in at him. He couldn't recall her ever having spoken to him before. She did now.

"Your poor eye," she said fretfully.

"It's nothin'," he grunted. "Just a shiner."

"Ezra couldn't have done that," she frowned. "He wouldn't anyway."

"I'm a real mean Hargrove," he growled. "I hit Cobb and Cobb hit me. Anything else you want to know?"

"Libby, honey, you oughtn't pester that young man," Nora chided over her shoulder.

"It's all right," murmured Libby. "We're just talkin'." She studied Chuck intently. "You want to know what Doc Sharman once told my pa?"

He wanted to rebuff this persistent girl, wanted to aim a hostile glare at her, but couldn't quite manage it. Gruffly he asked, "What?"

"A man oughtn't smoke lyin' down — specially in bed," said Libby. "It's bad for him."

"Well, pardon me all to pieces," he sneered.

"You're full of hurt and anger," she observed, "else you wouldn't talk that way to me."

"I got plenty of anger in me, sure, and I got good reason," he declared. "You know who I am, so you ought to savvy how I feel."

"I declare I'll never understand why cattle folks and farm folks can't be friendly neighbors," she sighed. "Everybody got to have beef. That's why cattlemen are important. But did you ever eat a steak with no greens on the side, no potatoes, no carrots or pumpkin? So who d'you suppose grows vegetables and the corn and the wheat for the flour? Farmers are important

158

too, but I guess you don't think so."

He eyed her warily and complained, "You and my sister — and all the other women — all thinkin' they're smarter than us men."

"Ain't tryin' to be smart," she shrugged. "Only tryin' to tell you how it ought to be." As she turned away, she flashed him a sad smile. "I won't bother you any more."

"You don't bother me," he muttered. The Greggs stayed another 10 minutes with Ezra. He farewelled them affectionately, cheerfully, his broad grin a fixture until they were moving out of sight, his father and sister toting the chairs. The connecting door closed. He frowned across at Chuck and remarked, "That was rough. I sure hope they don't do it again."

"You mean — your folks visitin' you?" challenged Chuck.

"Bad for 'em," sighed Ezra. "They don't belong in no jail, even as visitors. I could see Ma was nervous all the time. Pa made like he was real steady, mighty sure everything'd turn out right, but I can tell he's frettin'. Listen — uh — I hope Libby didn't faze you. She talks a lot, but she don't mean no harm."

"Your sister couldn't faze me," growled Chuck. "Here or anyplace else."

Ezra returned to his bunk, confused. Chuck Hargrove's retort had seemed downright defensive, almost desperate.

While Cobb opened up to let the Greggs out, the farmer addressed the Texans quietly, but firmly.

"This has to be said. If you can guard Ezra safe, keep him alive from now till he stands trial, there'll be no interference from Council Valley."

"We aim to do that, Mister Gregg," Stretch assured him.

"But . . ." Gregg's expression hardened. "If I hear of any more cowboys makin' trouble in town, totin' hangropes and tryin' to raid this jail, it's for sure you'll see me again — me and as many Valley men as will stand behind me. We'll be comin' in to deal with those hate-crazy hotheads, to show 'em farmers can be just as tough as any pistol-totin' cattleman."

"I sure hope that won't happen." said Larry.

"You and me both," nodded Gregg. "If it does happen, you mind what I've said. Won't be farmers make the first wrong move." He took his wife's arm. "Time to go, Nora."

"I thank you for — doin' your best for my boy," murmured Nora.

"Our pleasure, ma'am," said Stretch. "And my duty."

"Sheriff Emerson, you're my favorite of every sheriff I ever saw," enthused Libby.

Her father gruffly voiced a reprimand. She took his other arm and, as quietly as they had arrived, the Greggs moved out, crossed the porch and descended to the wagon. Cobb made to lock up again and was forestalled by Larry.

"I'm leavin' too. Back in a little while."

"Where you headed now?" demanded Stretch.

Larry didn't answer until he had crossed the threshold and sidled along to the open window. Cobb secured the door and, through narrowed and thoughtful eyes, watched the farmer help his womenfolk aboard.

"Got another minute?" he called.

As Gregg returned to the porch, Stretch and the jailer positioned themselves on their side of the window, curious as to what Larry would say to the farmer.

"Your boy's gonna need a lawyer," he warned.

"Been thinkin' about that," frowned Gregg. "It ought to be a Keever lawyer, one who knows this territory and the people. But there's only that high-toned Rossiter. He'll side with the Hargroves for sure."

"There's one other jasper — name of Peach," offered Larry.

"Only Peach I know of is a barber," protested Gregg.

162

"He's the one," nodded Larry. "Got discouraged and quit. But he's still a regular lawyer, got all the book-learnin'. I was about to go see him. Figured I should talk to you first."

"Peach is a loser," muttered Cobb. "That's why he quit. He couldn't out-talk Rossiter or Floyd Clemenshaw, never won a case."

"Look at it this way," suggested Larry. "At least Peach'll savy how to explain Ezra's side of it, and that'll count for more than big speeches and tryin' to out-talk Clemenshaw. What's important is how the judge and jury hears the facts. Maybe Peach is good enough to handle that. Listen, I'll size him up. You got my word I won't try talkin' him into it 'less I'm sure he's got what it takes. So what d'you say?"

"The way things are," Gregg said grimly, "I can't say 'no' to any man wantin' to help Ezra. So — you go ahead."

He returned to the wagon, climbed to the seat and kicked off the brake.

The vehicle was turned and driven away from the county jail.

"I wouldn't let Peach shave me," growled Cobb. "He's likely no smarter with a razor than with his mouth."

"Thanks for the advice." Larry grinned wryly. "Guess I'll settle for a haircut."

6

The Retainer

UNDERSIZED, diffident Leon Peach was by no means Keever's busiest barber. In shirtsleeves, shaggy-haired and thin-faced, he was slumped in the swivel-chair used by his few customers, when the tall stranger loomed in the doorway and looked him over. After inspecting the sensitive face bowed over the open book, the eyes pale blue and earnest, the nose straight, the mouth slightly droopy at the corners, Larry moved in, bared his head and, with his usual accuracy, tossed his Stetson to the hatrack. It settled firmly and Peach sprung to his feet and laid his book aside.

"Yes, sir! You're next and what's your pleasure?"

"Haircut," grunted Larry, lowering

his bulk to the chair. "Not too much off the back and sides. Business slow, huh?"

"It fluctuates," said Peach.

"I'll bet," said Larry, who had never heard that word before.

"Stranger in town," observed Peach, as he tucked the hair-cloth into his client's shirt-collar.

"And I'm a cattleman sometimes," nodded Larry. "But not right now."

"No," frowned Peach. "Now you're what might be called an unofficial deputy to our new sheriff."

"News travels fast in Keever," remarked Larry.

"My customers talk," shrugged Peach.

"I like to listen — got plenty patience," Larry assured him. "If you feel like talkin' about the case against young Ezra, go right ahead."

"My wife disapproves of my lingering affection for the legal profession," Peach confided. "So I must speak softly. Of course the case interests me. You may find this hard to believe, Mister . . . ?"

"Valentine," said Larry.

"Mister Valentine, incredible as it may seem to you, I was and still am a lawyer," declared Peach.

"I'll be doggoned," said Larry.

"Unfortunately, I was less than successful in this town," said Peach. "One must earn a living as best one can. I have a family to support, which is why you find me reduced to this somewhat lowlier profession."

He clipped and snipped and Larry drawled an assurance and hoped it was no lie.

"You're doin' fine."

For a while, Peach held forth on various aspects of the circumstances of Dacey Hargrove's death and the arrest of Ezra Gregg, proving he was well and truly acquainted with the basic essentials. Larry drawled a question, but casually.

"So — just supposin' *you* were defendin' Ezra — how would you handle it?"

"I would vigorously protest any claim

167

of murder, not that I believe Judge Mayo would support it." Warming to his subject, Peach talked on. "Also, I would challenge a manslaughter charge. Confound it, in a street-brawl, is one adversary striving to kill the other? If that were so, every pay-day cowhand involved in a saloon fracas these past several years should have been arrested for attempted murder instead of for disorderly behaviour. It's just not reasonable, you see."

"I'll buy that," said Larry.

Deftly, Peach tidied his right sideburn. "I would also dispute the cause of death and, though I admire him tremendously, challenge Doctor Sharman's ability to accurately state the same," he declared.

"Doc wasn't in his surgery when Dacey died," Larry said calmly. "He was away lookin' for his eye-glasses, him and his wife both. Only men with Dacey were Rossiter, McNear, Floren and a Broken Arow waddy name of Nicholls."

Peach paused to frown at him.

"Are you absolutely sure of that?"

"Wouldn't doubt the little lady's word — meanin' Doc's wife," said Larry. "And that's what she told me a while ago."

"So, although he was required to sign a death certificate, Doctor Sharman was not actually on hand when . . . "

"Uh huh. Mrs Sharman said Doc'd never swear Dacey died of the bump on his head."

"Excellent!" breathed Peach. He resumed his snipping — excitedly — much to his customer's disquiet. "The four who *were* present at the moment of death would never be acceptable as expert witnesses. Mister Rossiter is a lawyer — as I'm only too well aware — and the other three are cattlemen. By George! Myron Sharman's testimony would be invaluable to the defense, his wife's also. Excellent!"

"There's somethin' else, but maybe it won't help," said Larry.

"I'd be interested to hear . . . " began Peach.

"For what it's worth, Ezra's a mighty puzzled young feller," offered Larry. "The way it looked to him, Dacey didn't hit that wall so terrible hard. He can't savvy how Dacey could die of it, even though he was knocked out."

"A conclusion on the part of the defendant," said Peach. "Interesting, but inadmissable. I'm quite sure Judge Mayo would sustain an objection from the prosecution." He sighed heavily. "The prosecutor will be Floyd Clemenshaw — so I don't envy the poor devil retained as defense counsel."

"Clemenshaw got you spooked?" prodded Larry. "Rossiter too?"

"I have learned to my sorrow," said Peach, "a man should acknowledge his limitations. Against lawyers of the calibre of Clemenshaw and Rossiter, I'm quite ineffectual."

"Still and all," Larry said slyly, "It's the evidence that counts, right? If the defender got his facts all straight, he could still maybe impress a jury — no matter if the prosecutor talks smarter and louder."

"And Judge Mayo is a fair man," muttered Peach.

"Didn't burn your licence, did you?" challenged Larry. "Listen, how'd you like to get back into harness?"

As though that question were her cue, Constance Peach thrust the curtain of the rear doorway aside and made her entrance. She was passably attractive albeit a trifle on the buxom side, red-haired and assertive, her voice very firm, her whole demeanor suggesting she could never be talked down.

"My husband appreciates your offer, sir, but regrets he must decline," she informed Larry. "He is now a barber and no longer interested in legal matters — right, Leon?"

Peach's narrow shoulders sagged in defeat.

"Right, Constance dear."

"The children are home from school," she announced. "When you have attended this gentleman, kindly remember how you enjoy testing them on the day's lessons. We'll be waiting in the kitchen."

"Yes, Constance dear," said Peach.

She showed the impassive Larry a smile, half-gracious, half-triumphant, turned on her heel and marched back to her kitchen. Sad-eyed, Peach began working on Larry's neck-hair. He spoke very quietly now, very quietly indeed.

"You can see how it is, Mister Valentine. My wife has answered for me."

"Has she?" frowned Larry.

"Please, no more talk of the trial," begged Peach.

"Mightn't be a trial," Larry pointed out.

"I know about that," nodded Peach. "Most regrettable — not to mention barbaric — the demands of hate-ridden cattlemen — determined to lynch the defendant. I wish you and your friends every success in your efforts to defend the county jail against such . . ."

172

"I didn't mean what I said," muttered Larry. "Forget it. Don't ever doubt there'll be a trial. If *every* Verde Flats gun came a'raidin', we'd hold 'em off."

Barber and client lapsed into uncomfortable silence until Larry's dark thatch was trimmed to his satisfaction. Peach applied talcum, whisked the cloth away and was duly paid. He dropped the coin into his cashbox and tensed as Larry remarked, "She'd sure be surprised — and she'd have to change her tune."

When Peach turned, Larry was digging out his wallet.

"Don't tempt me!" he gasped. "Constance would never . . . " His eyes widened. Larry had extracted a banknote. "That — that's a fifty dollar bill!"

"What's called a retainer, I think," said Larry. "I wouldn't know the regular fee for a defense lawyer, but I'm ready to make you an offer. And don't be frettin' about this bankroll.

Every dollar we got, we came by it legal."

"Oh, hell!" groaned Peach. "I couldn't face Constance!"

"Be three more of these," said Larry, offering the money. "You collect another hundred and fifty after it's over — no matter how it ends."

"Two — hundred — dollars . . . ? blinked Peach.

"That enough?" asked Larry.

"Very . . . " Peach swallowed a lump in his throat, "very generous."

"Take it," urged Larry. "You'll figure how to square it with Mrs Peach. I'll pass the word to the sheriff and you can go talk to your client any time you want."

Peach's hand trembled as he took the bill from Larry and tried to fold it. He ended up stuffing it into his pants pocket.

"I can't promise anything," he softly warned. "Within the hour, don't be surprised if I return the retainer. If you had a wife like Constance . . . "

"Real fine lady," opined Larry, rising and reaching for his hat. "And no fool. You can use the money. Remind her of that, and she'll come round."

"Don't go, for pity' sake!" hissed Peach. "Back into the chair — quickly! I need time to — think about this. Won't get a chance when I confront her, so I'd better have everything clear in my mind. *Please*, Mister Valentine!"

Larry shrugged resignedly, tossed his hat to the rack and returned to the chair. He winced uneasily as Peach poured water into a mug and reached for a shaving brush.

"Uh — I don't need a shave — specially the way you're shakin'."

"Only two services you can buy here," mumbled Peach. "Haircut or shave or both. We have to talk. If she came in again and — we were only talking . . . "

"All right," sighed Larry. "But careful with the razor. You'll be shavin' the only throat I got."

"And, if I can summon the courage

175

to defy Constance, I'll also be defying the entire Verde Flats faction and two-thirds of the townfolk," fretted Peach, as he began lathering Larry's face. "The Hargrove influence is powerful, believe me. Why, this town was little more than a cluster of shacks until Rand Hargrove and Burch McNear drove a seed-herd onto the Flats twenty-four years ago."

"You know a whole lot about Diamond Seven, huh?" frowned Larry. He braced himself as Peach took up the razor. "How come?"

"When I arrived a couple of year ago with my wife and small children to hang up my shingle, I made a point of learning all the local traditions, the history of this country," said Peach. "A lawyer has that much in common with the local doctor, you know. He needs to know all there is to know about the territory and its people. McNear is younger than Mister Hargrove . . . "

"I noticed," said Larry.

He relaxed a little and mentally gave thanks; Peach was applying his razor with infinite care.

"Mrs Hargrove is younger again — almost a decade · her husband's junior, I believe," muttered the almost ex-barber. "Actually, both of them courted her. I learned that from some of the older folk."

"Who — what . . . ?"

"Auld was her maiden name. She was the only daughter of Keever's first telegrapher, long since dead. Yes, apparently Hargrove and McNear were rivals for her hand. Friendly rivals, I imagine. Well, if McNear stayed on to help run the ranch after his friend and Sophie were married, one assumes he took his loss like a gentleman."

"You know anything about this Jerry Floren hombre?" asked Larry.

Constance reappeared at that point, frowning suspiciously.

"Leon! The children!"

"As soon as I've shaved Mister Valentine, Constance dear," mumbled Peach.

"You were about to leave, I think,"

she accused Larry.

He was equal to that challenge.

"Sure enough, ma'am. But you shamed me."

"I did what?" she challenged.

"Plain truth is I don't always remember to shave, Mrs Peach," he said humbly. "Planned on havin' just a haircut — till I saw you. Lady like you. Me needin' a shave. You're the kind of lady reminds a man of his manners, and I thank you for that." He tried a disarming grin. "Pardon me for sayin' it, but your husband's my idea of a mighty lucky man."

"I've always thought so," Peach said bravely.

Completely taken aback, his wife made herself scarce for the second time. Peach started on Larry's other side.

"Floren? We're not acquainted. He's just another local rancher as far as I'm aware, though not a Verde Flats man. I understand his property is located . . ."

"Down by Council Valley," said Larry. "Yeah, that's what I heard. Listen, I got another question. How d'you figure a highclass professional gent like Rossiter turned out to watch Dacey and Ezra mixin' it? He don't seem the kind who'd socialize with just a few ranchin' men."

"I suppose he just happened to be with McNear at the time," shrugged Peach. "He's courting Miss Selma Hargrove, you see, so naturally he's acquainted with the Hargrove foreman."

"I guess that's it," agreed Larry.

Mercifully, Peach accomplished the task of shaving him without scarring him for life; he was profoundly grateful and said as much. Also insisted on paying again, though Peach protested the shave was not the customer's idea. Watching Larry don his Stetson, he grimaced uneasily and announced, "I'll have to — talk to her — at once. Have to get it over and done with."

"Do your damnedest," advised Larry, as he ambled to the street doorway.

179

"Last I heard, the husband's supposed to be head of the family and the wife vowed to love, honor and obey. Better think about that, Leon ol' buddy."

A few moments later, Peach entered the kitchen wearing the jacket of his suit and with his derby tucked under an arm. His children were seated at the table, their schoolbooks open, their expectant eyes on him. His wife turned from the stove and shook her head in vexation.

"Where could you be going now?"

"Emily — Henry — leave us please," said Peach. "You may retire to your rooms while your parents discuss a certain matter privately."

The youngsters promptly obeyed, leaving him to face his wife's intent scrutiny.

"I asked you a question," she sternly reminded him.

"I am going to the county jail," he announced. "I hope to be home in time for supper."

Her voice dripped icicles.

180

"And why, may I enquire, would you be going to the county jail?"

"To consult with my client," he declared. "I have agreed to defend Ezra Gregg against whatever charges are brought against him."

"You can't do that — can't go through it again!" she raged, eyes gleaming, cheeks reddening. "You said you'd learned your lesson after your last futile attempt to represent a client. Mister Clemenshaw — or any other lawyer — would make a fool of you! Leon, you *promised*!"

"Not voluntarily." He dared defy her now. "You browbeat me, Constance. You bullied me then — just as you're bullying me now — or trying to. Constance, can't you understand? I am haunted by my failures. I need this one last chance to prove myself. I may lose this fight as I lost all the others. But — *this* time — Floyd Clemenshaw will have to work harder for a conviction. *This* time, the court will remember me with respect! And, damn it, I may have reached a turning point in my career. I could even *win* this one!"

"You poor deluded fool!" she chided, as he began fishing out the $50.00 bill. "How can you be so muddle-headed as to believe you have any chance of . . . " Her voice soared to a yelp. "What is — that . . . ?"

"That is fifty dollars," he mumbled, tossing it to her. "More than enough to pay for Emily's new Sunday gown and the boots Henry so badly needs. May I remind you, Constance, I am still doing my best to provide for my family. That fifty dollars is my retainer. Win or lose — whether my client be convicted or acquitted — I am guaranteed another hundred and fifty, a total fee of two hundred dollars. But, Constance, I'd have accepted this brief for a fraction of that figure. I'd do it for *no* fee! Gratis! Nothing!"

"Now, Leon . . . " She was suddenly regaining her composure. "There is no need for such rash talk. You can only do your best and, if you feel so strongly about defending the Gregg boy, I'm sure you've made the right decision." The banknote was tightly folded and tucked into her bodice. "Hurry to your client. Do what you have to do — and I'll keep your supper hot."

"I was sure you'd understand," lied Peach, as he turned to leave.

★ ★ ★

That evening, around 7 o'clock, Larry quit the law office again, this time to visit the Appaloose Saloon. It was his intention to question members of the staff, barkeeps, table-hands, maybe the percentage woman, concerning Dacey Hargrove's baiting of Ezra Gregg the night of his death. All angles should be covered, he assured himself. It wasn't enough for Ezra to claim the fight had been forced on him; there had to be witnesses to back up that claim.

He was a half-block from his destination when his sixth sense told him he was being kept under observation.

He slowed his pace, resisting the impulse to glance over his shoulder. A few seconds later, a man shuffled out of an alleymouth to accost him and he recognized that same deadbeat, the permanently thirsty Ike Jeffers.

"Hey, friend, could you spare . . . ?"

Jeffers didn't finish his pitch. Firmly, but not aggressively, Larry had grasped him by his pants-belt.

"How'd you like a silver dollar?" he quietly offered. "All you got to do to earn it is . . . "

"You just name it, mister," Jeffers said eagerly.

"I got the feelin' somebody's taggin' me," muttered Larry. "Peek round my shoulder — casual — and tell me if anybody's gawkin' this a way."

The deadbeat obeyed, then squinted into Larry's face.

"Ain't nobody payin' you any mind — 'cept two fellers. Other side of the street. A little ways along."

"Would you know 'em?" demanded Larry.

"Oh — well — everybody knows them gents," Jeffers assured him. "One of 'em's Mister Rossiter, the lawyer. Other gent is Mister Floren, the Broken Arrow boss."

"Here you go, amigo." Larry pressed the coin into the anxious paw. "Don't spend it all in one place."

Jeffers shuffled away and Larry ambled on to the Appaloosa, nudged the batwings open and entered. En route to the bar, he was intercepted by a generously curved female in a gaudy red gown, who drawled the usual invitation.

"Well, hallo there, handsome stranger. You want to buy a lady a drink?"

"For a little co-operation, I'll buy you the whole bottle," he offered with a genial grin.

She gave him the fluttering eyelids routine.

"Whatever's your pleasure, honey."

"Were you here the night Dacey Hargrove prodded the farm-boy into a fight?" he asked.

At once she recoiled from him.

"I dunno nothin' about that."

Quickly, she moved away from him. He shrugged impatiently, strode across to the bar, found elbow-propping space and caught a barkeep's eye.

"Rye. Double shot."

The barkeep did his duty, accepted payment and was making change, when Larry put his question. Gruffly, the barkeep replied, "Sure, I was here, but I don't remember anything about it."

"C'mon now," chided Larry. "Who d'you think you're foolin'? Bartenders don't miss anything. You must've seen and heard Dacey fazin' the kid."

"Mister, I got nothin' to say to you," growled the barkeep.

"What're you afraid of?" challenged Larry.

"Ain't afraid of anything," the barkeep retorted. "But I plan on mindin' my own blame business, savvy? I'm here to serve booze — not to answer your questions."

"What can you lose by . . . ?" began Larry.

"Let up, will you?" The barkeep glowered at him. "What's the matter? You don't savvy plain English?"

"Take it easy," frowned Larry. "I'd as soon keep this friendly. But don't give me that kind of back-talk. It could cost you a couple teeth."

"Anything wrong here, Morty?"

This question was voiced quitely by the portly and dapper saloon owner. Rollo Dinsdale had advanced to Larry's left side and was eyeing him warily. Larry returned his appraisal while taking a pull at his whiskey.

"Stranger's pesterin' me," the barkeep complained. "Won't take no for an answer. Tryin' to make me talk about — you know what."

"What exactly?" Dinsdale asked Larry.

"Here's where it started," Larry reminded him. "The Gregg boy's in jail because young Hargrove was crowdin' him — right here."

"What's your interest?" demanded

Dinsdale. "Why buy into something that's none of your business?"

"None of my business?" Larry downed another mouthful and studied both men. "The hombre wearin' the last sheriff's badge is my partner. He's set his mind to holdin' Ezra for a fair trial — and I feel the same way. You still claim it's none of my business? Every man's got a right to his day in court. Or maybe you don't believe that? Better to let a lynch-mob have him?"

Dinsdale shrugged resignedly and muttered an order to the barkeep.

"Answer his question, Morty."

"You sure I should do that?" challenged the barkeep.

"Old Rand wouldn't approve," said Dinsdale. "But we have no choice, Morty. You know what a subpoena is?"

"Never heard of it," mumbled Morty.

"I'll explain it as simply as I can," said Dinsdale. "Judge Mayo goes by the book, everything fair, square and legal. A subpoena is an order. You can be ordered to attend a trial and give evidence. They could serve a subpoena on me too, on every man and woman working for me. And maybe they will. So answer the question."

"All right," scowled Morty. "It was Dacey started it. The sodbuster kid was drinkin' beer and keepin' himself to himself. I'll allow he wanted to — uh — stay away from Dacey. But Dacey kept after him, called him yellow, went right on cussin' him."

"That's how it was," Dinsdale assured Larry. "Any of my tablehands, any of the girls would have to say it that way. Morty, I'll have what the Texan's having." He picked up the glass filled for him by the barkeep and nodded an invitation. "Be my guest."

Larry followed the saloonkeeper to his private table. They seated themselves and Larry accepted a Havana cigar, never suspecting he would not be given time to finish it. He half-emptied his glass, lit up and traded stares with his host, who said softly. "It's awkward for us, Mister . . . ?"

"Valentine."

"Valentine, I'm Dinsdale. And, when I say awkward, I'm not fooling. Sure, we'll testify, and that'll make the Appaloosa a mighty unpopular saloon, far as the Verde Flats trade is concerned."

"You sayin' Hargrove could close you down?" prodded Larry.

"I don't know if he'd go that far," said Dinsdale. "He wouldn't need to send his hired hands to start a ruckus and wreck the place. He'd only need to spread the word, blackball me, and you'd never again see a rancher or any of his hired hands in the Appaloosa. A lot of townmen, my regulars, would follow their lead, not wanting to run foul of Diamond Seven — you understand?"

"You make it real clear." Larry finished his whiskey and grinned mirthlessly. "It'd be better for busines if cattlemen did bust Ezra out of jail and hang him. No trial at all."

"I'd like you to believe I don't want *that* either," frowned Dinsdale. "That's why we're having this private conversation, Valentine. I want to be sure the new sheriff knows where I stand."

"So you ain't for lynchin'?" asked Larry.

"Ever see a lynchin'?" countered Dinsdale.

"Any time my partner and me came on a lynch-party, we broke it up — one way or another," Larry said coldly. "That's how *we* feel about a hangin' with no trial."

"I've seen it happen in another town and I have to agree with Billy Keele, our mayor," said Dinsdale. "A good town is never the same after a lynching. There's a lousy atmosphere thereafter, know what I mean? I saw a town die of shame, Valentine."

"Any town that'd let it happen deserves to die," growled Larry.

"That's how it was with Kermoyle

Gulch, Colorado," said Dinsdale. "It's just a ghost town nowadays. Well . . . " He frowned moodily at his untouched drink. "Now you know my feeling. If the kid lives to stand trial — and I hope he does — you won't need to have us subpoenaed. The owner and staff of the Appaloosa will be there anyway, ready to tell the truth as we saw it."

"I'm obliged," nodded Larry, rising. "Tell Morty I'm sorry I had to lean on him."

He walked out of the saloon with the half-smoked Havana canting from the side of his mouth and crossed Main Street. Pre-occupied with his thoughts, he began sauntering. He was in the block where his and Stretch's horses were stabled, passing the mouth of the alley this side of Kennedy's Barn, when a gun barked from the other side of the street, the dark alley directly opposite. An oath erupted from him as the tongue of fire lashed at his right side, the impact of the bullet throwing him off-balance.

He sprawled in the alleymouth, rolled over and slid his Colt from leather. From the opposite alley his attacker fired again and, by then, his gun-arm was extended and his Colt cocked. He aimed for the gunflash and squeezed trigger so quickly that the two shots merged as one. High and clear, he heard a yell of agony. That cry was followed by the subdued, urgent sound of receding footsteps. Squinting, he saw the two figures briefly silhouetted at the far end of the alley, one aiding the other. He had scored sure enough. They disappeared to the right and, a few seconds later, he heard the clatter of hooves. They were riding now, headed southeast.

The first local to reach him, as he began lurching to his feet, was old Johnny-On-The-Spot himself — Ike Jeffers again. Upright and plagued by pain, Larry holstered his Colt and grabbed at the deadbeat. The thud of booted feet on plank side-walks warned him others were converging on the scene.

"You're about to earn another dollar," he said tersely, and he slid the coin into a pocket of Jeffers' tattered vest. "When the busybodies start hollerin' questions, tell 'em I'm dead."

"But — you ain't," protested Jeffers.

"I'm buyin' time!" snarled Larry.

"You got it," nodded the deadbeat.

Retreating to the rear of the alley, Larry stumbled around the corner to move through the back doorway. The stablehand gaped at him; from 3 inches below his right armpit, all the way down to the knee, his clothes were wet with blood.

"Saddle the sorrel," he urged. "Do it fast!"

While the stablehand hustled to ready the animal, Larry investigated the clutter in the cubbyhole left of the rear entrance. He found a half-full bottle of whiskey, pulled the cork, tugged his upper garments up to his armpits and doused his wound. The sting of the raw liquor on torn flesh caused his eyes to water. Through a red haze of pain, he trudged to the sorrel. The stablehand secured the cinches and, laboriously, he struggled astride. He tossed a coin and started his mount quick-stepping to the rear doorway. Out front, locals were excitedly questioning the deadbeat, unaware the sniper's victim was on the move.

"He's dead!" Jeffers announced for the fourth time.

"You keep sayin' that," a townman impatiently complained, "But *who*, damn it? *Who's* dead?"

"George Washington," frowned Jeffers. "Died Seventeen Ninety-Nine. Hell. I thought *everybody* knew that."

From the edge of town, Larry swung southeast. He made it to a trail and pushed on, pain-hazed eyes probing the moonlit terrain ahead. Maybe he wasn't bleeding now; he had no way of knowing. But the agony was still with him. His cursory inspection of the wound indicated it was some 3 inches long, a straight slash, mercifully shallow. And now, unless he fainted from loss of blood, he would ignore that wound and stay after the fleeing riders if only long enought to identify them.

At the law office, with the three gunshots still echoing along the street, Stretch had reacted instinctively, to be promptly forestalled by the grim-faced turnkey.

7

Witness In Hiding

COBB positioned himself with his back to the locked and barred street-door, watched Stretch dash to the gunrack for a rifle and growled, "Forget it."

"What d'you mean, forget it?" mumbled Stretch. "I'm sheriff, ain't I? Some fool starts a shootout in this town, I gotta bring him in!"

"You're a real nice feller, Stretch, and I like you fine," said Cobb. "But you ain't as smart as your partner."

"Never have been," Stretch admitted. "You think I don't know it? Always, it's been Larry did all our figurin'. I just go along."

"Well, be smart now," advised Cobb. "Don't go along out of here. Anywheres outside the county jail, you're a target. All the law we got. Only badge in

197

Keever. Can't you smell a trap when it's laid for you?"

"You sayin' them shots was a trick?"

"To draw you into the street. They'll down you one way or the other, Stretch. If you don't get a bullet in your back, you'll be jumped and gunwhipped so bad you couldn't remember your own name — let alone protect your prisoner."

"That was a dumb notion," sighed Stretch, replacing the Winchester, returning to his chair.

"Don't feel bad about it," Cobb consoled him. He made for his favorite doss, the ancient leather-covered couch. "Pooley would've run out too." Scathingly, he added. "Back when he had the guts for it."

"I sure wish Pooley hadn't quit," sighed Stretch. "I ain't right for this kind of work, Newt. Too much responsibility. Too damn many things I got to think about. And thinkin' makes my head hurt." He remarked with some relief, glancing to the cellblock door. "I'm real glad Mister Peach got through talkin' to Ezra and left before the shootin'. He looks like a loser, the kind who'd be unlucky enough to stop a wild slug."

"I calculate Peach was home and half-way through his supper when we heard those shots," offered Cobb.

"That's a mercy," shrugged Stretch. "He don't look much, but he's the only lawyer Larry could find for Ezra."

"I guess Peach'll do his best," grimaced Cobb. "Only trouble with Peach's best — it never does anything for the poor jasper in the shackles."

"Got to be a first time for everything, Larry always says," recalled Stretch.

"I'm sorry, but I got to say it," frowned Cobb. "If Peach puts up a strong fight for the kid, this'll be one mighty surprised town. They say his wife bosses him all the time. A man takes too much of that, it kills his spirit."

"Comes the trial, we'll have to put some spirit into Peach," opined Stretch.

"Even if it comes out of a bottle."

Two hours later, though still in pain, Larry was congratulating himself. At his last pause, his keen ears had caught the distant thud of hooves. He had proceeded less than 100 yards when, clear in the moonlight, he spotted the riders. They had to be the same two; one was slumped low in his saddle. From behind a rockmound, he watched them quit the trail to enter a straggle of brush. Patiently he waited, listening. The hoofbeats ceased.

He dismounted, ground-reined the sorrel, unfastened his spurs and hung them to the saddlehorn. To the brush he crept, hugging all the cover he could find. Light flashed briefly within the brush, suggesting somebody had scratched a match. It proved something, that brief show of light. His quarry were unaware they had been followed.

The voices were audible when he reached the near edge of the brush. Audible enough? He cocked an ear and a mumbled reprimand reached him clearly, followed by the angry retort.

"Quit your whining, damn it. Hold still while . . ."

"Easy for you to talk, Jerry. *I'm* totin' a bullet. Not *you*!"

"No bullet in you, Rudy. Told you, didn't I? He only grazed you. But you sure settled *his* hash. I just *know* we're rid of that nosey Texan. You got him with your second shot."

A wail of pain was followed by Rudy's gasped protest.

"The booze is makin' it worse — feels like my whole arm's afire!"

"Want to keep that arm, don't you? The whiskey'll kill infection. When we make Broken Arrow, George'll finish what I've started. We got everything you need, pal. Bandage, ointment, everything. Couple days in your bunk and you'll be good as new."

"But I'll still have that chill in my gut, Jerry. Oh, hell. What we did to Hargrove's boy . . ."

"I told you to forget it, you fool!"

"Can *you* forget it?"

"I've forgotten it already. Got better to think about."

"Yeah, sure. Gold. You and McNear and the lawyer . . ."

"And you, Rudy. And George and Beau. We all end up rich, don't forget that. Plenty for all of us."

"If Hargrove runs the farmers out of the valley."

"He will, Rudy, he will."

"They still ain't raided the county jail."

"What difference? What do we care if the Gregg kid lives to stand trial? What if he's acquitted? That'll only make Rand madder. There'll be bloody war in the valley. We only have to wait till the last sodbuster quits, then Cousin Arnie'll draw up the papers and us mining speculators'll own all the valley land — and all we can dig out of it."

There was a long pause. Larry leaned forward, disciplining himself to control his mounting fury. When Rudy spoke again, every word reached him with chilling clarity.

"Did Dacey have to die that way? Did we have to go that far — sink that low?"

The other man chuckled harshly.

"Don't mourn for Dacey. He's feeling no pain now. He was just a pawn in the game, Rudy. It was a golden opportunity for us. How could we pass it up — a chance to turn Hargrove against the whole Council Valley community? Young Gregg is the perfect patsy."

"And you'll go on trustin' that bastard McNear? Oh, sure, we held Dacey down on that table when he looked like comin' to his senses, you, me and Rossiter. What we did was lowdown, Jerry, but what McNear did — I never saw anything like that before and I'm never gonna forget it."

"You have to admit, Rudy . . ." The other man was chuckling again. "It couldn't have been easier."

"McNear enjoyed it, damn him! Enjoyed clampin' a hand over Dacey's mouth and pinchin' his nose so he couldn't breathe — so he smothered . . . !"

That outburst was checked by the two sharp sounds, a hard slap and Rudy's cry of pain.

"*Now* will you quit whining?"

"Don't — ever do that again — Jerry. You ever hit me again — you better be ready to use a gun!"

"You were damn near hysterical. Come on now, the bleeding's stopped. I'll help you mount and we'll get you home."

Larry stayed quiet, squatting on his heels, hand on gun-butt. He listened to the sounds that followed, a grunt of pain, the clink of a spur, then the hoofbeats. When the two horsemen passed him, he was holding his position, barely concealed by dry brush; neither man glanced his way. He watched them move back to the trail and swing southeast again.

Not until they were well and truly out of sight and earshot did he struggle upright. The effort started his head swimming and his legs almost gave way. He waited a long moment, then started for the rockmound and the waiting sorrel, feet dragging, wound throbbing, senses reeling. Twice he fell. The second time, sprawled face-down, he spat dirt and cursed his nausea. It wasn't that deep a wound, he reminded himself. But the bleeding. Damn and blast. He thought he had checked the bleeding.

"Must've leaked a couple pints — or more," he fretted. "This is fine. Just great. Anybody finds out I tagged 'em to here, they'll spook and run. That's no good. Got to make it back to town."

He made slow work of drawing a knee forward and raising himself. Swaying, staggering, he labored on to the mound and around it, there to lift his rein and a boot to stirrup.

"You stay real still, boy. Let me flop now, move before I'm ready — and I'll be all through."

Grasping the saddlehorn, missing the wheel of a spur by less than an inch, he loosed a startled oath.

"It won't look right. Why would I take off my spurs? If McNear's in town — if he sees me — he could guess. Damnit to hell!"

He drew his boot from stirrup, detached the spurs and retreated to a flat rock to squat. In his weakened condition, it took him better than 5 minutes to re-fasten his spurs. Then he faced up to the heavy chore of rising and returning to his horse. Again he grasped the saddlehorn. He clenched his teeth, fitted boot to stirrup and hauled himself up and over, the effort almost causing him to keel to the other side. He straightened up, got his other boot into stirrup and, as he began wheeling his mount, assured that trusty animal.

"It's for sure we ain't gonna hustle. This is gonna be slow — real slow."

Later, he was to wonder how he made it back to Keever's Main Street and the area in front of the law office. He lost track of time.

Had he lost consciousness too? Hell, no. How could an unconscious man stay mounted? Now he disciplined his blurring vision, doggedly defying his weakness. In the light of nearby street-lamps, he was in clear view of the people hurrying toward him. They saw him dismount painfully, remarked on his bloodstained clothing as they drew nearer. A moment before he flopped to his knees by the steps leading up to the porch, he recognized Arnold Rossiter; the lawyer was thrusting himself to the fore. A blackgarbed man, Reverend Abner Wallace, questioned him. Loud enough for all to hear, he delivered his brief speech.

"Some sonofabitch took a shot at me. I tried to follow him but — fell off my horse — about fifty yards out of town. Passed out. Came to my senses — scarce had strength enough to get mounted again . . . "

"Trying to ride in your condition was a serious mistake," chided the parson.

207

"Be grateful your horse brought you back."

"Plain truth is . . . " groaned Larry. "I don't feel real — grateful — right now . . . "

He closed his eyes and sprawled against the steps. The law office door opened and Stretch came bounding out. Cobb followed, brandishing a shotgun and ordering the area cleared, demanding the doctor be summoned. The people dispersed, all but Rossiter and Burch McNear, the latter having arrived in town just an hour ago. These two retreated to the opposite sidewalk.

When Larry opened his eyes, he was on the office couch and stripped to the waist. Stretch had also tugged off his boots and relieved him of his gunbelt. Cobb was watching from his vantagepoint at the window while the aged Doc Sharman, balding and stoop-shouldered, hovered over the patient, squinting through his spectacles as he secured the bandage wound about the brawny chest.

"Considerable loss of blood, I'd say." The voice was quavery, but the hands deft. "The wound — not too serious. I'll replace the dressing tomorrow afternoon."

"Okay if he stays here, Doc?" asked Stretch.

"If you can keep him quiet," frowned the medico. "And well-fed. That's important, you understand. Plenty of nourishment to compensate for the loss of blood." He nodded reasurringly to his now wide awake patient. "You'll heal, young feller. But you should stay off your feet a couple of days."

"Doc, there's somethin' you got to do for me, and it's mighty important," muttered Larry.

"Just relax," soothed Sharman. "Clear your mind of all worries and . . . "

"I've been wounded before," growled Larry.

"Many times," nodded Sharman. "Yes, I could not fail to observe the old scars on your chest and your back, your arms too."

"Anybody else been in here since I passed out?" Larry damanded.

"Nope," grunted Stretch. "Just us and Doc."

"That's fine — just fine," breathed Larry. "Now, Doc, you listen good. I don't want it known I'm in good shape. It'll be better for young Ezra if everybody thinks I'm hurt bad, maybe dyin'."

"Better for Ezra?" Sharman blinked perplexedly and glanced to the cellblock door. "If you're assumed to be in a critical condition, this would be favorable to the Gregg boy?"

"You got to admit you already got a bad feelin' about the way Dacey Hargrove died," said Larry. The old healer's face creased into a hundred tiny furrows; he suddenly appeared even older.

"I have — certain reservations," he said softly.

"I ain't askin' you to lie, because I know you doctors got rules," said Larry.

"We are required to abide by a code of ethics," nodded Sharman.

"But, if anybody asks, do you have to say Valentine's fine, be up and around in three-four days?" challenged Larry.

"It might help," Sharman gently suggested, "if you could be specific, tell me exactly what you expect of me."

"You don't have to say much at all," Larry assured him. "Just give 'em a sad look — real serious — maybe shake your head. Say you did your best for me, then shrug — kind of helpless."

With the vaguest hint of a grin, the old doctor remarked, "You ask me to be devious. That's quite a challenge — and against my better judgement."

"For the right reasons, you could do it." opined Larry.

"And the right reasons are . . . ?" prodded Sharman.

"I can make this territory breathe easy again," declared Larry. "It's a powderkeg right now, every citizen's

211

spooked, fearin' there'll be war 'tween cattlemen and farmers and a lot of good men killed on both sides."

"That is the prevailing atmosphere," frowned Sharman. "A sorry situation. A threat to the peace and security of us all."

"I can change all that," promised Larry. "If I can lay low till the trial, then show up to testify, the things I say will change everything. There won't be any more cattleman cravin' to raid Council Valley, nor any more farmers plannin' to stampede raid on Verde Flats."

"You will present yourself as a surprise witness?" demanded Sharman.

"That's the way I want to do it," delcared Larry. "Right there in the courthouse — the only place ranchers and farmers'll have to sit and listen. If I told what I know right now, it wouldn't be the same."

"You have — certain information?" asked Sharman.

"And I'll be tellin' everything I

know," nodded Larry. "But it has to be at the right time and in the right place."

The medico studied him a long moment, then nodded.

"Very well. I'll be discreet and, if necessary, devious."

"No matter who asks," stressed Larry. "No matter how well you know 'em — and trust 'em."

"Tight secrecy?" frowned the medico. "It's that important? This promises to be a very interesting trial." He closed his bag and, as Cobb opened up for him, showed Larry a reassuring grin. "You made a very favourable impression on Adela. I don't quite understand what you hope to achieve, but I'll certainly co-operate."

When Sharman had left, Larry sat up and began re-donning his blood-stained garments. Impatiently, he enquired, "Who's cookin' my supper?"

The aged healer crossed Main in his usual hesitant way, wary of passing horsemen and vehicles. On the opposite sidewalk he was accosted by Rossiter and McNear.

"Good evening, Doctor." The lawyer greeted him respectfully. "We couldn't help noticing that unfortunate Texan . . ."

"Looked like he was shot up bad," remarked McNear.

"Ah, yes," sighed Sharman.

"Was he able to offer the sheriff a more detailed report of — whatever happened to him?" asked Rossiter. "I know he was shot near Kennedy's Barn and, before he collapsed in front of the sheriff's office, I believe I heard him say he had attempted to pursue his assailant, but fell from his horse a short distance from town."

"There was little more he could tell the sheriff, I'm afraid," said Sharman.

"He gonna die, Doc?" demanded McNear.

The medico assumed a doleful expression while wracking his brain. How to answer so blunt a question and honor his promise to his burly patient? Inspiration came to his aid. Nobody lives forever. He turned to McNear, shrugged helplessly and declared, "He will die, I regret to say. Yes. It's only a matter of time."

His questioners traded quick glances. Rossiter frowned and said, "I'm extremely sorry. I'm not acquainted with the man, but I'm extremely sorry."

"Yeah," grunted McNear. "I'm sorry too."

Cobb faced the prospect of being deprived of his favorite resting place, but wasn't about to complain. He busied himself at the stove after Stretch fetched food from the cell that had become their pantry. They were being patient, figuring Larry would take them into his confidence, but only when he was good and ready. He didn't talk until he was half-way through his meal.

"I have to deal you two in," he muttered. "But that's just in case somethin' happens to me. And, when I'm through talkin', you keep it to

215

yourselves, savvy? If our secret broke, the killers'd cut and run and Ezra would still be a target for every hothead cattleman hereabouts."

He repeated the damning converstion on which he had eavesdropped, confining himself to the gist of it, telling it tersely and very quietly. They reacted pretty much as he expected, Cobb launching an outburst of shocked profanity, Stretch shaking his head incredulously.

When he regained control of his feelings, the turnkey recalled an almost forgotten rumor.

"This means McNear never forgave old Rand," he said in disgust. "I happen to know both of 'em courted Sophie."

"Back when she was Sophie Auld," nodded Larry.

"You know about that?" frowned Cobb.

"Heard it from Peach," said Larry.

"We save it all for the trial, huh runt?" prodded Stretch. "Yeah, I see the sense of that. Everything out in the

216

open. It'll be rough on Hargrove, but he'll have to believe it."

"You'll testify," guessed Cobb.

"Couldn't be a better way of setting things to rights," opined Larry, trading rueful grins with his partner. "What d'you say, stringbean? Quite a change for us?"

"We never had much respect for the legal way of doin' things," Stretch said wistfully. "Always went by our own rules — till now."

"This is one of those special times." said Larry. "With the Verde Flats crowd and the Council Valley farmers near ready to make war, we have to handle this right."

"By the law," agreed Stretch.

"Strictly between us three," Larry cautioned Cobb. "Not a word to Ezra."

"How about the barber — I mean the lawyer?" asked Stretch.

"I'll have to deal him in," decided Larry. "But not right-away. Later. When it's time to go to court."

"And, meanwhile, this town better

believe you're done for," said Cobb.

"That'll be easy enough," said Larry. "You have somebody stable my horse. I'll stay right here till the day of the trial. Anybody comes visitin', you don't let 'em in till I'm bunkin' in a cell by the rear door."

He was weary by the time he finished that substantial meal, but convinced he would be restored to full strength in ample time to strike his decisive blow against the conspirators of Keever County.

★ ★ ★

Toward noon of the next day, at about the same time a telegraph message was delivered to the sheriff's office, Selma Hargrove came to town again. News of the shooting had reached Diamond Seven and she was eager to visit the victim. To avoid another quarrel with her father, she used the excuse of taking her jailbird brother a change of clothing.

The telegram advised the new sheriff that Circuit-Judge Mayo's schedule provided he would arrive in Keever earlier than expected, day after tomorrow. Larry was undismayed and said as much.

"We'll all be ready. Specially me."

Cobb announced Selma's approach from his position at the window and Larry decided against retreating to a cell. After she was admitted, Stretch and the turnkey should go check on the prisoners, leaving him to talk to her in private.

"Talk?" frowned Cobb. "Well — uh — how much would you tell *her*?"

"Won't be doin' much tellin'," growled Larry. "But, when I'm through talkin', she'll know better than to shoot off her beautiful mouth. Count on that."

A tattered blanket was drawn up to his neck when she arrived. Cobb re-secured the door. Stretch took the spare clothing from her and offered to give it to her brother while she sat with the patient a while. He placed a chair by the couch, beckoned Cobb and unlocked the cellblock door. Cobb followed him into the jailhouse, closing the door behind him.

Seated by the couch, studying Larry's impassive face, the blonde beauty softly declared, "I am desperately sorry to see you in this condition, Larry."

"I ain't all that happy about it," he muttered.

"But you do look better than — than I expected," she said with a puzzled frown.

"I'll heal," he assured her. "But do me a favor, Selma. It has to be a secret. What some people don't know can't hurt me — you know what I mean?"

"You have a reason for this?" she challenged. "For letting everybody assume you're at death's door?"

"Soon enough, you'll know my reason," he promised. "Now, Selma, you got it all. The best-lookin' woman in this territory is the best-educated — so you ought to be the smartest.

But you're still a woman, and women like to talk."

"Men can be just as talkative," she countered with a good-humored smile. "But we won't argue about that."

"I'd as soon you told nobody about this," he said bluntly. "About findin' me lookin' healthier than you expected. Selma, I'll be countin' on you, understand?"

"If it's so very important, naturally I'll guard my tongue," she murmured.

"I said nobody," he frowned. "Best friends, family — includin' kid brother Chuck — nobody at all."

She studied him intently.

"Suddenly I feel as though I were holding a bible in my left hand and raising my right," she complained. "Are you swearing me to secrecy?"

"I though I was makin' that clear enough," said Larry.

"You've made it very clear," she nodded. "And you may rely on my discretion. Now could we be friendly?"

"I got a question," he drawled. "If

we're friends, you won't get mad."

"Ask then," she invited.

"You got any ideas of marryin' your lawyer friend?" he demanded.

For a moment, he was sure she resented that personal question. She surprised him by shrugging nonchalantly.

"That's in the future. I haven't decided. Arnold is very attentive, very ardent, but I'm in no hurry. I'd need to know a man a great deal longer than I've known Arnold before I'd consider him as a marriage prospect."

"But you like talkin' to him?"

"Why, certainly. He's a good conversationalist."

"You happen to remember if you talked about me, last time you saw him? You were meetin' him for lunch as I recall, and it was right after you and me traveled from Diamond Seven together."

"Well, yes, I did mention you. Is there any reason I should not have?"

"You talk about my notion of

checkin' with Doc Sharman — and all that?"

"You don't mind, I hope? You didn't confide your intentions as a secret. Arnold was quite impressed, described it as a very interesting theory, the possibility of Doctor Sharman administering the wrong medicine."

"I don't mind, Selma," said Larry. "I was just curious is all. Only — from now on . . . "

"It shall be as you wish," she promised. "Not a word to a soul — including Arnold."

"And, if anybody asks, you mind lyin' on my account?" he grinned.

"How big a lie?" she challenged.

"I'm low, real low," he said. "Mightn't last another day."

Her face clouded over.

"Larry, are you anticipating another attempt on your life — by the same man? He'd try it again, if he learned you weren't seriously injured?"

The right answer would seal her lips, he decided.

"It could happen," he nodded.

"Then I'll be careful," she fervently declared. "Terribly careful, Larry."

"Good girl," he said approvingly. "Go on now. Go visit kid brother."

Selma Hargrove spent 15 minutes with a somewhat reticent younger brother. The change in him was obvious to her, but she deemed it wise to refrain from direct questions. Not once during their conversation did he mention the other prisoner; Ezra had borrowed dubbin and a cloth from the turnkey and was squatting on his bunk, trying to put a shine on his shabby boots. She flashed him a smile. He nodded politely and went on with his chore.

"Thanks for the clean duds, sis," Chuck acknowledged, when she rose to leave.

"Anything else you need, just ask," she offered. "And, by the way, your eye is improving."

"Both of 'em," he said softly.

"And what does *that* mean?" she wondered.

"I'm seein' a little clearer," he muttered. "Been doin' a lot of thinkin'. But I don't want to talk about it."

"All right, Chuck, I won't ask you to explain," she smiled.

Before being ushered out by Cobb, she was informed by Stretch that Judge Mayo was now expected day after tomorrow, some time before sundown.

"I figured you ought to know," he explained, "so you can tell — everybody that's interested."

"Judge'll want to hold court the next mornin'," predicted Cobb.

"I suppose we should all be thankful the judge is arriving so soon," she remarked, trading stares with Larry. "The sooner the trial, the less danger of further assaults on this jail."

By mid-afternoon of that day, the news had spread to every corner of the county. Concerned parties began speculating on the outcome of the trial and, at the Verde Flats spreads, there was less talk of ways and means of breaching the defenses of the county jail. Now there was talk only of the coming trial and much conclusion-jumping as to how 'that jelly-livered barber' would suffer another humiliating defeat at the hands of the spell-binding Floyd Clemenshaw.

After supper, an apprehensive Leon Peach presented himself at the county jail for another conference with his client.

"I expected to find you in a coma," he told Larry. "Your wound is supposed to be mortal, according to all the rumors. The bullet too close to the heart for Doctor Sharman to attempt probing for it. You've made your will and given instructions regarding the inscription on your gravestone."

"Is that what folks're sayin'?" grinned Larry.

"Mister Peach, suh, you just forget Larry's lookin' so chipped," urged Stretch. "What he wants is for folks to keep right on thinkin' what they're thinkin'."

"That he's near dead?" frowned

Peach. "Well, if this would be any advantage . . ."

"It will," Larry assured him. "Now go parley with Ezra and, the night before the trial, there'll be another parley. Just you and me."

Later that evening, one of Keever's most distinguished citizens approached the law office and was recognized by Cobb.

"The county prosecutor himself," he announced. "Floyd Clemenshaw. You want to use that end cell now?"

"Might be better," nodded Larry, rising from the couch. "Tell him to wait, then you two carry me inside. Got to make it look good."

"Yeah, sure," agreed Stretch. "A little play-actin' for the prisoners."

Wrapped in a blanket, Larry was toted to the end cell and laid gently on the bunk, Ezra and Chuck watching, but refraining from comment. After all that effort, the austere, hatchet-jawed Clemenshaw did his talking from the open street doorway, and tersely.

"You'd have to be formally notified," he told the new sheriff. "In the case of Keever County against Ezra Gregg, my colleague Arnold Rossiter will act as prosecutor. I've received word of the sudden illness of a relative and have to start for the San Marco railhead at once. But you needn't be concerned, Sheriff Emerson. Mister Rossiter has all the ncessary information and is well-qualified to act on the county's behalf."

Informed of this change, Larry grinned coldly and declared, "I wouldn't have it any other way."

Late afternoon, two days later, Judge Roy Mayo's familiar surrey was stalled outside the Palace Hotel. The time of reckoning was at hand.

8

Case For the Defence

HE was a rotund, jovial jurist, almost 50 years old, but wearing his years well. And still Peach was overawed by Judge Mayo when, at his invitation, he visited his hotel room with the substitute prosecutor.

"Too bad the new sheriff couldn't join us," Mayo remarked. "However, according to the hotel manager, Sheriff Emerson doesn't dare leave his office. There have been threats of lynching?"

"I'm afraid so, Your Honor," nodded Rossiter.

"Appearing for the defense again, hey Mister Beecher?" smiled Mayo. "After a temporary retirement from practice."

"Peach, Your Honor."

"My apologies, Mister Peach. It's

been so long. Well?" Mayo eyed Rossiter enquiringly. "Dare I hope this case can be settled in one day? I propose we begin at nine-thirty. Clemenshaw was kind enough to supply a written account of all the known facts, so, unless one of you resorts to delaying tactics . . . "

"Straightforward case, Your Honor," shrugged Rossiter. "We should finish mid-afternoon, maybe earlier. You agree, Peach?"

"Well . . . " began Peach.

"I hope it's understood a charge of murder could not be accepted," said Mayo.

"Manslaughter?" frowned Rossiter.

"Under the circumstances, more appropriate," nodded Mayo. "I believe there was a second arrest, but Clemenshaw made no mention of it."

"Sheriff Emerson has decided not to proceed with the charge against Charles Hargrove, brother of the — uh — hapless victim of . . . " mumbled Peach.

"Yes, yes, I recognized the name," said Mayo. "And now, gentlemen, if there's nothing more . . . " He grinned his genial grin, "I'll see you in court. All right? No foreseeable hitches?"

"I think not," smiled Rossiter. "We have ample time for notifying the Hargroves and Greggs and all witnesses. I'm sure Mayor Keele will arrange for couriers to carry the word."

Returning to the law office, sweating profusely, Peach sagged into a chair and doggedly assured the Texans and the turnkey, "I'll regain my nerve when the trial begins. Don't worry about me. I intend to work hard for young Ezra."

"Well, I'll tell you, Leon ol' buddy," drawled Larry. "It ain't gonna be so rough for you this time. You just sit quiet, listen to me a while and, when I'm through, forget what I've said till you call me to testify. From then on, you leave everything to me."

"I don't understand," protested Peach. "You — a witness for the defense?"

231

"Don't ask dumb questions, Peach," chided Cobb. "Just listen."

Peach listened with his jaw sagging and his eyes bulging while, quietly, compellingly, Larry reported his pursuit of his would-be assassin and the Broken Arrow boss. The substance of the conversation he had overheard was repeated as accurately as he knew how, after which Peach had to be fed a stiff shot of whiskey.

There was little sleep for Peach that night. His spouse seethed with curiosity, but not one word did he confide to her. Excitement kept him awake, the certain knowledge that, on the morrow, he would win his first case in Keever — if only because of Larry Valentine's Lone Star luck.

The Verde Flats people arrived early; most of the cattlemen, their families and a strong representation of their hired hands were in town by 8.30 next morning. But they arrived no earlier than the farmers of Council Flats, whose vehicles blocked the area in front of the jailhouse. Marvin Gregg climbed to the porch and moved to the window for a brief parley with Stretch.

"If you're ready to trust my people, we're ready to give you safe escort to the courthouse," he announced. "How are you plannin' on movin' my boy from here to there? It's a block and a half, Sheriff."

"Horseback," said Stretch. "Me and Newt ridin' flank."

"We'll lead you," offered Gregg. "We'll be in back of you too and at both sides. That way, no hothead ranch-hands'll get in spittin' distance of you."

"You got a deal," Stretch said cheerfully.

At 8.50, Cobb entered the jailhouse and ambled to Chuck Hargrove's cell, jingling a keyring.

"Get dressed, young feller," he ordered, as he unlocked the cell. "Sheriff's droppin' all charges against you and turnin' you loose."

Rising, Chuck surveyed him warily. "You wouldn't josh me, would you?"

"Sheriff got the idea you've grown up some since you started fillin' this cell," drawled Cobb. "Got to say I agree with him. You're cured of lynch-fever, right?"

"Right," sighed Chuck. "But I don't deserve a break."

Cobb swung the door wide.

"Come to the office when you're ready to collect your stuff."

"Cobb, I'm sorry I tried to hit you," declared Chuck.

"Well, I ain't apologizin' for clobberin' you," grinned Cobb. "Black eye kind of straightened you out, huh?"

"I reckon I needed that," said Chuck.

A few moments later, he stepped out of the cell, toting his extra clothing and trading stares with Ezra, who grinned wistfully and remarked, "Lucky you."

"Do somethin' for me," begged Chuck.

"*Me* — do somethin' for *you*?" Ezra

asked uncertainly.

"I'd sure appreciate it," muttered Chuck. "Ain't likely I'll get close to your sister today, close enough to say what I want to say, but maybe they'll let you talk to your family before the trial."

"So?" prodded Ezra.

"Tell her somethin' for me?" frowned Chuck. "When she talked to me the other day, I wasn't real sociable, forgot my manners. Will you tell her I'm sorry about that and I beg her pardon?"

"I'll do that," promised Ezra.

"I'll bet neither of us figured I'd end up sayin' this to you." Chuck sketched him a salute. "Good luck today, Ezra. And I really mean that."

In the office, while pocketing his personal effects and strapping on his gun, he glanced to the blanket-covered man lying on the couch, eyes closed. After thanking Stretch for dropping the charges, he asked about the other Texan and was told by Cobb, "It's hard to say."

"Maybe he'll live and maybe he won't, huh?" prodded Chuck.

"That's about the size of it," nodded Stretch. "C'mon, kid, I'll let you out the back way, give you a boost over the fence. Too many farm folks out front. You goin' to the trial?"

"Well," said Chuck, "I thought I'd wait outside the court-house for my folks."

At 9.10, when Stretch and Cobb emerged from the office with their prisoner, the assembled farmers aimed warning stares at the people on the sidewalks. There was no challenge, no uproar, when they walked Ezra down to the waiting horses. As they mounted, they were hemmed in on all sides by farmers and their hired hands, all mumbling encouragement to the self-conscious Ezra.

Not until the escorting officers, their prisoner and the heavy force of Council Flats men reached the courthouse did the uproar begin. Verde Flats men were out in force, bellowing abuse,

236

denouncing Ezra, yelling threats.

"You'll hang anyway, farm-boy!"

"And that's a promise . . . !"

"We already found you guilty, farm-boy! We got the rope — and we'll choose the time!"

At 9.30, Larry thrust his blanket aside and, unhurriedly, donned his boots. Time was what he had plenty of, he assured himself. He got the stove working, set the coffeepot in position and wandered into the jailhouse to fetch a bottle of whiskey from the supply-cell. While waiting for the coffee to boil, he seated himself at the desk. The street-door was locked from the outside, the shade drawn on the window; he had privacy.

Court was in session, a jury now being impaneled and Judge Mayo wondering why none of the men selected were challenged by Peach. Prim in his Sunday suit, the defense attorney sat beside the defendant with Stretch and Cobb directly behind. The court-room was jam-packed, the

Hargroves and Greggs occupying reserved seats in the second and third rows. Already the temperature was rising; it promised to be an uncomfortably warm day and all side windows were open, crowded with locals who had arrived too late to get inside.

Larry took his time ejecting the shells from his Colt, helping himself to oil and cloth from a drawer of the desk. The weapon was cleaned, oiled and its mechanism tested by the time the coffeepot began chattering. He rose and sauntered to the stove, flexing his muscles en route, working his right arm. The wound was healing well and, since being carried into this office, he had worked hard at regaining his strength, eating regularly and with gusto. He filled a cup, two-thirds coffee, one third whiskey. Carrying it back to the desk, he took a sip, then slowly reloaded his Colt and slid it into the holster.

Arnold Rossiter was now delivering

his opening address, Hargrove listening intently and grimly studying the defendant's profile, Gregg trying to conceal his dismay; the jurors were townmen, most of them known supporters of the local cattlemen. In good form, Rossiter eulogized the late Dacey Hargrove and sternly vowed justice would be done this day. The prosecution would leave the jury in no doubt as to the manner of Dacey's passing and the guilt of the accused.

Then came the parade of witnesses, first Jerry Floren, then his employee Rudy Nicholls, a mite pallid and moving carefully, then Burch McNear. Thrice the side alley brawl was described, and not until McNear had offered his testimony did Peach see fit to cross-examine. Seated in the rear of the court, his wife braced herself.

"Now it comes," she assured herself. "Now he'll strive so hard to show confidence, poor, dear foolish Leon."

"I challenge only one detail of your testimony," said Peach. And, to his wife's astonishment, he spoke firmly. "You stated — twice I believe — that the defendant was ready for this fight. Those were your exact words, were they not? Gregg was ready for it, you said?"

"That's what I said," nodded McNear.

"I'll be calling witnesses, the owner and staff of the Appaloosa Saloon," warned Peach, "people who saw and heard the decedent goad my client — deliberately — until he felt compelled to accept a challenge to fight, rather than be branded a coward. Ezra Gregg was ready for this fight? Do you still persist in that assertion? Really, Mister McNear, would it not be fairer to say the decedent was ready — far more so than the defendant?"

"When the Gregg farm-boy finally made up his mind, he was good and ready to fight Dacey," growled McNear.

"Thank you," said Peach. "No more questions, Your Honor."

"You're satisfied with the last answer,

Counsellor?" frowned Mayo.

"Quite satisfied, Your Honor," said Peach. "I believe I have made my point."

McNear was ordered to stand down. And now, while Dr. Myron Sharman tottered to the witness-box to submit to Rossiter's questioning, Hargrove spoke quietly to his son and daughter.

"That milk-sop Peach is gettin' nowhere. Dacey's killer is as good as convicted."

"Don't gloat," Selma softly pleaded. "Not at a time like this."

"Somethin' ailin' you, boy?" Hargrove challenged Chuck. "You've scarce said a word to us since you met us in front of the courthouse."

"I'm fine, Pa," said Chuck.

"And properly grateful to Sheriff Emerson, I hope," murmured Selma.

"Yeah," grunted Chuck. "Grateful — and a whole lot wiser."

While the aged medico answered Rossiter's questions, Mayo grimaced often, fidgetting, shifting in his chair.

Irritably, he demanded the witness raise his voice for all to hear. Sharman did his best.

"Let me be sure I understand, Doctor," Rossiter said sternly. "Can there be any doubt in your mind as to the cause of death? Surely — considering the decedent's condition when we brought him to your surgery — it is obvious the head-wound inflicted by his assailant would prove fatal?"

"I must object, Your Honor!" called Peach, rising.

"Don't just object," Mayo curtly chided. "You know the rules, Counsellor. Elaborate, but with brevity if you please. Clarify your objection."

"I object to the prosecutor's use of the words 'inflicted' and 'assailant.' Certainly the decedent reeled from a blow struck by the defendant. He then fell against a wall and, as other witnesses have testified, the impact caused the head-wound." Peach eyed Rossiter reproachfully. "And 'assailant' is hardly the right term. 'Adversary' would be more appropriate."

"Objection sustained." Mayo was fidgetting again. "Doctor Sharman, do you recall Mister Rossiter's last question?"

"I do," nodded Sharman. "And I repeat I am at a loss to explain the decedent's sudden death. I say sudden because, as I left the surgery to look for my spectacles, he was showing signs of reviving. As to the cause of death — seizure, heart failure, shock or whatever — I would not swear the head injury was potentially fatal."

"My apologies, Doctor," Rossiter said smoothely. "This questioning must be distressing to a man of your years." He turned away. "Your witness, Mister Peach."

"Just one question, Doctor," said Peach. "When you left your surgery for your spectacles — the decedent being alive at that time — you were accompanied by Mrs Sharman?"

"I was," said Sharman.

"Thank you," said Peach. "No more questions."

"Next witness?" asked Mayo.

"The prosecution needs no more testimony, Your Honor," said Rossiter. "The facts speak for themselves, and I'm sure the gentlemen of the jury are in no doubt as to the defendant's responsibility for . . ."

Mayo used his gavel and winced and, now, a great many people were intrigued by the change in him. It seemed to have happened suddenly, the usually urbane and genial judge so ill at ease, so cantankerous.

"Enough, Counsellor!" he sharply chided Rossiter. "Your witnesses have been heard — following your opening address. Your next address, the closing of the prosecution's case, will afford you ample opportunity for such remarks. Now is not the proper time."

"Of course," nodded Rossiter.

Larry finished his spiked coffee, rose to his feet and strapped on his Colt. He thonged the holster down, donned his Stetson and decided his time had come. His nerves were rock-steady, all his self-assurance intact; he was as ready as he would ever be.

Letting himself out by the rear door, he moved across the jail yard, collecting an empty barrel en route to the fence. He used the barrel as a booster and easily hauled himself over the fence, then made for the courthouse.

Avoiding the packed front entrance, he shouldered his way to a side window. Locals watched and listened from there, three deep. Thanks to his generous height, he could see part of the area in front of the bench including the witness-box. Peach was rounding off his opening address to the jury.

" . . . ill-feeling and hysteria — better described as fanatical hostility to the young man facing judgement today. Never in the history of Keever County has an accused man been so victimized by prejudice. But now you will learn the truth, gentlemen of the jury — now you will hear testimony — more than testimony — *hard proof* — that Ezra Greg is innocent of any intent to do more than defend himself . . . !"

"Brevity, please," interjected Mayo. Taken aback, Peach turned to frown at him.

"I beg your pardon, Your Honor. My opening address . . . "

"Yes, yes . . . " The judge grimaced and writhed. "I don't mean to inhibit you, Counsellor. However . . . "

"I had just about concluded my opening remarks anyway," said Peach. "I will now call my first witness. That is, if Your Honour will permit the defendant to take the stand. Under the usual conditions of course. My client understands Mister Rossiter is entitled to cross-examine, but this does not dismay him. His conscience is clear."

"The defendant will take the stand," muttered Mayo. "Orderly, you will administer the oath."

Shoulders squared, his clean-shaven face impassive, Ezra took the stand, placed his left hand on the bible, raised his right and swore to tell the truth. Peach then urged him to recount the events leading up to the fight in the alley. He did so hesitantly, grudgingly, recalling the belligerence and persistence of his challenger, going on to describe the fight in simple terms.

"You are uncomfortable," frowned Peach.

"Well — yeah — I sure ain't enjoyin' this," muttered Ezra. "It's — uh — it's speakin' ill of the dead. And that ain't right is it?"

"Unfortunate, but necessary," said Peach. "One final question. You were shocked — quite incredulous in fact — when told of Dacey Hargrove's death?"

"Couldn't believe it at first," shrugged Ezra.

"Why not?" demanded Peach. "You fought him. You have a clear recollection of that brawl. Why was it so difficult for you to believe he had died?"

"It's like I've been sayin' all along," frowned Ezra. "To me, it didn't seem like he hit that wall hard enough to hurt himself so bad — and die of it."

"Thank you," said Peach. "Your witness, sir."

He retreated while Rossiter rose and advanced on the sad-eyed Ezra.

"Remember you are under oath," was Rossiter's opening thrust. "And answer yes or no! Is it not a fact that you hated Dacey Hargrove — as you hate all cattlemen?"

Mayo had to use his gavel again; hot-tempered cattlemen were volunteering answers at the full strength of their lungs. He threatened to order the court cleared, then nooded to Ezra to answer the question. And Ezra answered it unflinchingly.

"I don't hate cattlemen nor anybody else. Hate never did any good for any man. That's what my folks taught me, and that's what I believe."

"You bitterly resented the decedent's remarks to you in the saloon," accused Rossiter. "When you accepted his challenge, it was your intention to

248

punish him, to inflict pain, to kill . . . !"

"Objection, Your Honor!" protested Peach. "My colleague is deliberately haranguing the witness!"

"And he should know better!" Mayo was restless again, seemingly incapable of sitting still. "Mister Prosecutor, ask specific questions or . . . !"

"I have no more questions," shrugged Rossiter.

"You may stand down," Mayo told Ezra. "Next witness?"

"The defense calls Lawrence Valentine," announced Peach.

With that, Lary made an unconventional entrance, clambering through the side window. He removed his Stetson as he made for the witness-box and, over the rumble of excited comment, called an apology to the bug-eyed Mayo.

"Sorry, Judge. Couldn't make it through the front entrance."

Mayo mumbled something unintelligible and nodded to the court orderly. Larry took the oath and gave his name.

All eyes were on him now, but he was oblivious to the gaping of the Verde Flats and Council Valley factions; right now he was only interested in the reactions of a half-dozen men, Rossiter, McNear, Floren and the three hired hands of Broken Arrow.

"Your Honor, anticipating the prosecution's objections to my preliminary questions," said Peach, "may I offer assurance that relevance will be well and truly established? What befell this witness does have a bearing on this case."

"Very well, Counsellor, but *get on with it!*" gasped Mayo.

He mopped at his sweating brown and writhed again but, whatever the cause of his distraction, listened intently to Peach's first question.

"Are you fully recovered? A few nights ago, you suffered a gunshot wound, is that so?"

"I was creased," nodded Larry. "Feelin' fine now, thanks."

Though he kept his eyes on Peach,

he was certain Rossiter, McNear, and Floren were trading covert glances.

"Will you kindly tell the court of your actions immediately following the attempt on your life?" Peach politely requested.

"Well, sure," said Larry. "I had the stablehand saddle my horse, then I rode out after the sidewinder that shot me. I was pretty sure I creased him with a bullet, figured he wouldn't travel very far, the shape he was in. But he had help. There was another man with him."

"How far did you follow these men?" asked Peach.

"All the way to the brush where they waited a while," said Larry. "They talked — and I got close enough to hear 'em."

"And so, unaware they had been followed, unaware they could be overheard, these men talked freely?" prodded Peach.

"They sure did," Larry said grimly.

"Repeat, please, exactly what was

said," urged Peach.

His jaw sagged. Mayo was banging with his gavel, silencing him. He turned to frown at the judge. So did Larry and everybody present.

"We'll hear the rest of this witness's evidence after the lunch recess, Counsellor," Mayo said quickly.

"Your Honor . . . !" Peach hastily consulted his watch. "The time is — only quarter after eleven — surely too early for . . ."

"Don't back-talk me, Counsellor!" rasped Mayo. "We will resume in one hour!" He used his gavel again. "Sheriff, take charge of your prisoner. Court's adjourned!"

As the courthouse began emptying, Larry caught Stretch's eye and nodded to the six men joining the crowd making for the main doorway. Stretch returned his nod and drawled a command to Cobb.

"You stay here with Ezra. It's too early to eat anyway, and he'll be safe enough here."

"Well — uh — where you goin!?" demanded Cobb.

"Larry and me got a chore," said Stretch, moving away.

For their means of exit, the Texans chose Larry's means of entry.

"What the hell?" frowned Stretch, as they dropped from the side window. "How come the judge stalled you — right when . . . ?"

"I said enough to spook 'em," growled Larry, leading him to the main stem. "And now they'll vamoose — if they can."

Reaching the front of the courthouse, they stared over the heads of the dispersing crowd and, almost immediately, sighted the six. They were moving toward a livery stable, Rossiter clutching Floren's arm and talking urgently, McNear obviously enraged.

"I got ten bucks says them hombres' aim to ride," offered Stretch.

"No bet," said Larry. "You circle around back of the barn and, if we have to use our guns, you flop — muy pronto. I wouldn't want to blow a hole through you."

"Well, shucks, I sure appreciate that," retorted Stretch.

Moments after the six entered the barn, Larry reached the street doorway, Stretch the rear. The stablehand came hustling out, intimidated by McNear's curt dismissal. He moved past without noticing Larry, who stood poised to one side of the entrance, ears cocked, hand on holster.

"Hearsay evidence . . . !" Rossiter was pleading. "At least give me a chance to discredit Valentine in my cross-examination. Jerry — Burch — I can do it!"

"You can't do a thing, cousin," growned Floren.

"Plain enough, ain't it?" challenged McNear. "He heard it all and there's no way we can stop him. Only thing we can do is run while we can. We're all through in this territory. We have to forget the gold — forget the whole deal."

Haunted by his guilt, his wound still plaguing him, Rudy Nicholls was voicing his fears when Larry stepped into the doorway. Rossiter, Floren and McNear were grouped with Nicholls in the passage between the stalls. The other men, Prentice and Waincott, had elected to saddle the horses; they were moving in and out of stalls to either side.

"I aim to be long gone," Nicholls assured the lawyer, "when Rand Hargrove finds out what we did to his boy."

"It's your word against Valentine's, don't you see?" challenged Rossiter. "Yours and Jerry's. And you're local men. You can deny everything and, when I face up to Valentine, I'll make a fool of him, show him up as a muddle-headed saddletramp!"

"Well," said Larry. "You could try."

The four whirled to stare at him. Prentice promptly emerged from a stall with hand on gun-butt. Waincott ducked out of sight, but not fast enough to escape the attention of the taller Texan looming in the rear doorway.

McNear's face contorted.

"Minute I laid eyes on you," he coldly declared, "I got the feelin' I'd have to put a slug in you some day."

"Listen, we daren't waste time," muttered Floren. "By himself, Valentine can't stop us. Rudy — George — take care of him!"

"Rudy didn't do so good last time," warned Larry. "I think he got the worst of it."

To the accompaniement of a stamping of hooves, Waincott now reappeared. He was mounted and hustling a charcoal colt into the passage, turning it towards the rear doorway.

"The hell with it, Jerry," he called over his shoulder. "I ain't just *talkin'* of goin'. I'm goin' — right *now*!" Sighting Stretch barring his way, he yelled a warning. "Hey! There's two of 'em . . . !"

His impulsive move triggered a chain reaction of violence and bloodshed. His gun cleared leather fast but, by then, Stretch had emptied his holsters. They fired almost simultaneously, almost but not quite. Waincott's Colt boomed a split second after Stretch's first bullet slammed into his chest; he was toppling when his gun discharged, blowing a hole in the barn roof. Rossiter, panic-stricken, sidestepped as McNear drew on Larry. Floren, Nicholls and Prentice promptly filled their hands, the latter two turning to shoot at Stretch, who threw himself flat with his arms extended, his Colts leveled.

Drawing and dodging, Larry felt the airwind of McNear's bullet. He returned fire and, as the rogue ramrod collapsed, turned his gun on Floren. The lawyer's treacherous kinsman was making a fatal mistake, frantically striking the hammer of his Colt to send his bullets whining toward Larry. Fanning a Colt, even at that short range, was flashy and futile, the action causing the muzzle to move with each shot. He fanned three that sped over Larry's head before Larry shot him down.

In that wild exchange, a bullet had seared the rump of the riderless black. Crazed with pain, the animal nickered shrilly and reared, forelegs threshing. Again Rossiter sidestepped, but not fast enough. A flying hoof struck his head. He flopped, dazed, and then both forehooves came down on him, pounding.

Stretch yelled to the animal from his prone position, his matched .45's blazing at Nicholls and Prentice. Hastily, Larry dropped to his knees. He need not have worried. Stretch's fast-triggered slugs traveled no further than his targets. Nicholls cried out and went down with his right shoulder bloody. Prentice loosed no yell of pain. He died on his feet, gun slipping from his quivering hand, blood trickling from his mortal wound. When he collapsed, the horse stomped Rossiter again, reared again, then charged forward. Larry darted into a stall and watched the charcoal race past and out into the main street.

Among the first townmen to converge on the scene of carnage were the mayor and the preacher. At Larry's urging, they joined him beside the anguished, pain-wracked Nicholls.

"You guessed, huh?" he challenged. "When I started givin' evidence . . . ?"

"Oh, hell!" groaned Nicholls. "You heard — every damn word we said . . . !"

* * *

"No tellin' how long you'll last, Nicholls," warned Larry. "If I was shot up so bad, I wouldn't count on too much help from a sawbones as old as Doc Sharman. I'd be wantin' to wipe my slate clean."

* * *

"All *their* idea . . . !" Nicholls blurted it out to Keele and the parson. "Jerry and Rossiter — they were blood-kin. I dunno how they found out about — the gold — in the creek that runs through the valley. But they decided they'd have to — see every sodbuster forced out. And, when we toted Dacey into Doc's place and Doc and his wife left us, that was their chance. I'm still sick from — what we did . . . "

He described the murder in almost the same words he had used when discussing it with Floren in the brush, shocking Keele and Wallace to the core.

"And now my parnter'll put him in a cell and send for the doc," muttered Larry, eyeing them steadily. "I'll finish my testimony . . . "

"Yes," sighed Wallace. "You don't have to say it. Mayor Keele will do his duty, and so will I. We've no choice but to repeat this man's confession."

"Any of the other's still livin'?" Larry asked Stretch.

"Not so you'd notice," muttered Stretch. "Hell! What that crazy horse did to the lawyer. Stove his head in. His chest too."

The trial was resumed in an atmosphere of tense expectancy. A relaxed and alert-eyed Judge Mayo reminded Larry he was under oath and ordered him to continue his testimony and, in blunt language, Larry repeated that damning exchange between Floren and Nicholls. At the end of it, not waiting for Peach's next question — Peach didn't have one anyway — he declared, "It had to be Rossiter gave the word for me to be killed, and now I savvy why. He learned I was askin' questions at the Sharman house about what happened to Dacey Hargrove. Plain enough he was leery of me, fearin' I was gettin' too close to the truth." Silence. Shocked cattlemen, farmers and townfolk were froze in their seats. He turned to address Mayo. "They're all dead, Judge. All but Nicholls, the one I scored on. He was hit again — and scared bad — so he said it all again."

"Counsel for the defense, if this can be substantiated . . . " began Mayo.

"Well, Your Honor . . . " shrugged Peach.

"Judge Mayo . . . " The mayor rose and approached the bench, tagged by Parson Wallace. "The Reverend and I can vouch for every word you've just heard. We were there when Nicholls confessed. So, if you'll have us sworn in, we'll gladly tell what we heard."

Fifteen minutes later, Mayo was ordering the defendant released from custody and energetically banging with his gavel, but in vain. The court was in uproar but, this time, outraged farmers and their hired hands were shouting the ranch-hands down, reminding them of their threats to lynch Ezra for what was now known to be murder, a murder committed by the Diamond Seven foreman with help from two other cattlemen and a scheming lawyer.

Mayo was despairing of quelling a riot when Marvin Gregg moved up to the bench to stand beside the judge's chair. His sudden appearance caused the clamor to die down long enough for him to beckon the shattered Diamond Seven boss and call an invitation.

"Rand Hargrove, will you join me and help me talk sense to all these damn fools? I figure it's up to us. So what d'you say?"

As he rose to his feet, Hargrove glowered about him and growled a warning.

"Next Diamond Seven waddy opens his yapper, he's off the payroll. And you other Verde Flats ranchers, if you got any sense, you'll give your men the same warnin'." He trudged through the wide-eyed crowd and up to the dais to stand on the other side of Mayo's chair. "Now you all listen to me. This is my day to eat crow. I lost a son and my grief was stronger than my reasonin'. So now we all know better, don't we? Now we know the whole lousy truth?"

"Maybe there's gold in Council Valley," Gregg said grimly. "And maybe us farmers that own the land will try pannin' for it. But that don't mean we're gonna quit plowin' and sewin' and raisin' crops. Try eatin' gold-dust and, by golly, you won't stay alive for long. It takes good food to keep a man alive and healthy, his women and young'uns too. Wheat, corn, greens and anything else we can grow." He turned to Hargrove as he added, "And beef."

"Damn right," nodded Hargrove. "And beef." He fixed a sad eye on the Council Valley men. "Listen now, I'll allow you got good reason for totin' a grudge, but you got to admit it takes two to make a fight. I'm apologizin' to Marv Gregg and his boy right here and now and, if he's got no objection, we'll shake hands. For the rest of my life, I'm gonna cuss myself for blamin' young Gregg for my son's death."

"You were used," declared Gregg. "I was used. Ezra too. We were too blind to see things clear, but now we know better, right?"

"Right," nodded Hargrove. "Now

we know better. So will you shake my hand?" As they shook, he eyed the farmers again, and his own men. "You savvy what this means? No more feudin'. I'll expect every Verde Flats man to follow my lead."

"And you Valley men better follow mine," growled Gregg. "Or you'll answer to me."

The uncomfortable silence that followed was broken by foot-steps and a jungle of spurs. Chuck Hargrove had risen from beside his mother and sister and was moving across to where the Gregg women sat. Watched by the dumfounded cowpokes and farmhands, speaking loud enough for all to hear, he took the seat vacated by Gregg and addressed Nora.

"Mrs Gregg, ma'am, I'd be honored if you and Mister Gregg'd permit me to call on Libby."

Judge Mayo beamed jovially as the rumble of comment began. Hargrove and Gregg traded resigned grins and Ezra, relaxed and cheerful, airily remarked, "That don't surprise me one little bit. When Libby and Chuck got to talkin' at the jailhouse, I could tell right off he was interested."

"This almost tragic crisis ends on a happy note," Mayo said amiably. He banged with his gavel. "Court's adjourned — and may this be the end of this ill-feeling between the cattle and farming folk of Keever County."

The courthouse began emptying. To the right of the main entrance, Constance Peach was waiting to congratulate her husband, her face wreathed in smiles. And Peach was eager to join her, but even more eager to satisfy his curiosity on a certain point. As Mayo left the dais, he confronted him.

"Judge Mayo, may I make so bold . . ."

"Something I can do for you on this happy occasion, Peach?" grinned Mayo. "Quite a triumph for you, huh? Not the last time you'll appear before me, I'm sure."

"Judge, I have to know," insisted

Peach. "It was without precedent, completely unexpected. I might even say outlandish. Your inexplicable decision to break for lunch at such an early hour . . . !"

"Lower your voice," begged Mayo, gripping his arm. "Please!"

Peach lowered his voice, talking softly, people jostling him en route to the exits.

"Do you now realize that, had Mister Valentine been given time to complete his testimony, all the guilty parties could have been apprehended right here in the courthouse — without bloodshed — without loss of life?"

"Don't rub it in," sighed Mayo.

"Why then?" demanded Peach. "Why interrupt Valentine's testimony — at that critical moment?"

"Because, young feller, I was in acute distress, couldn't wait another minute," muttered the judge. "I'll thank you to keep this to yourself. If it became known — well — it would be embarrassing for me, very embarrassing. You don't wish to cause me embarrassment, I take it?"

"Of course not," frowned Peach.

"So keep your mouth shut about this," ordered Mayo. He hesitated a moment, then confided, "It must've been something I ate at breakfast, or maybe supper the night before. Damn it, Peach, I had the most distressing bellyache and was frantic to get to a privy!"

"Good grief," blinked Peach.

"Don't laugh," scowled Mayo.

"I wouldn't laugh," Peach earnestly assured him. "It's too serious."

"Serious is an understatement," declared Mayo. "May it never happen to you, Peach. Think of it. You could be half-way through addressing the jury, interrogating a witness . . . "

"A harrowing thought," said Peach.

"Enough to start my bowels seething again." Mayo shuddered at the memory. "What do you say we forget it?"

Outside the courthouse, Larry spoke briefly with Selma. She was dry-eyed, shocked by the untimely death of the lawyer she had admired and trusted, but not distraught. Her voice was steady as she acknowledged, "I can be wrong about people — terribly wrong despite my studies in psychology."

"Happens to me all the time," he offered. "I don't always guess right about men like Rossiter and Floren. About McNear, I figured him for one mean hombre, but I'd never have believed he was Dacey's killer."

"All our lives, Dacey's, Chuck's and mine, Burch McNear was hating my parents, resenting the happiness they found together," she said bitterly. "They realize it now, Larry, but I pray God they'll clear their minds of such bitter memories." She summoned up a smile. "You, of course, are restless again. I won't be surprised to hear you and your friend have quit the territory. Feet itching already, Larry?"

"All that book-learning wasn't wasted," he grinned. "Here's *one* man you understand good."

Some weeks later exactly 25 minutes after the famous Bob Corlaine arrived in Keever and was sworn in by the mayor, the Texans saddled up and rode out. A mile south of the county line, Stretch sighed heavily and said, "Do us both a favor."

"Yeah, what?" asked Larry.

"Next time we're camped someplace and needin' supplies," said Stretch, "*you* go to town for 'em."

THE END

CALABOOSE EXPRESS
WHISKEY GULCH
THE ALIBI TRAIL
SIX GUILTY MEN
FORT DILLON
IN PURSUIT OF QUINCEY BUDD
HAMMER'S HORDE
TWO GENTLEMEN FROM TEXAS
HARRIGAN'S STAR
TURN THE KEY ON EMERSON
ROUGH ROUTE TO RODD COUNTY
SEVEN KILLERS EAST
DAKOTA DEATH-TRAP
GOLD, GUNS AND THE GIRL
RUCKUS AT GILA WELLS
LEGEND OF COYOTE FORD
ONE HELL OF A SHOWDOWN
EMERSON'S HEX
SIX GUN WEDDING
THE GOLD MOVERS
WILD NIGHT IN WIDOW'S PEAK
THE TINHORN MURDER CASE
TERROR FOR SALE
HOSTAGE HUNTER'S
WILD WIDOW OF WOLF CREEK
THE LAWMAN WORE BLACK
THE DUDE MUST DIE

TOP HAND
Wade Everett

The Broken T was big. But no
ranch is big enough to let a man
hide from himself.

GUN WOLVES OF LOBO BASIN
Lee Floren

The Feud was a blood debt. When
Smoke Talbot found the outlaws
who gunned down his folks he aimed
to nail their hide to the barn door.

SHOTGUN SHARKEY
Marshall Grover

The westbound coach carrying the
indomitable Larry and Stretch headed
for a shooting showdown.

FIGHTING RAMROD
Charles N. Heckelmann

Most men would have cut their losses, but Frazer counted the bullets in his guns and said he'd soak the range in blood before he'd give up another inch of what was his.

LONE GUN
Eric Allen

Smoke Blackbird had been away too long. The Lequires had seized the Blackbird farm, forcing the Indians and settlers off, and no one seemed willing to fight! He had to fight alone.

THE THIRD RIDER
Barry Cord

Mel Rawlins wasn't going to let anything stand in his way. His father was murdered, his two brothers gone. Now Mel rode for vengeance.

ARIZONA DRIFTERS
W. C. Tuttle

When drifting Dutton and Lonnie Steelman decide to become partners they find that they have a common enemy in the formidable Thurston brothers.

TOMBSTONE
Matt Braun

Wells Fargo paid Luke Starbuck to outgun the silver-thieving stagecoach gang at Tombstone. Before long Luke can see the only thing bearing fruit in this eldorado will be the gallows tree.

HIGH BORDER RIDERS
Lee Floren

Buckshot McKee and Tortilla Joe cut the trail of a border tough who was running Mexican beef into Texas. They stopped the smuggler in his tracks.

BRETT RANDALL, GAMBLER
E. B. Mann

Larry Day had the choice of running away from the law or of assuming a dead man's place. No matter what he decided he was bound to end up dead.

THE GUNSHARP
William R. Cox

The Eggerleys weren't very smart. They trained their sights on Will Carney and Arizona's biggest blood bath began.

THE DEPUTY OF SAN RIANO
Lawrence A. Keating and
Al. P. Nelson

When a man fell dead from his horse, Ed Grant was spotted riding away from the scene. The deputy sheriff rode out after him and came up against everything from gunfire to dynamite.

FARGO: MASSACRE RIVER
John Benteen

The ambushers up ahead had now blocked the road. Fargo's convoy was a jumble, a perfect target for the insurgents' weapons!

SUNDANCE: DEATH IN THE LAVA
John Benteen

The Modoc's captured the wagon train and its cargo of gold. But now the halfbreed they called Sundance was going after it . . .

HARSH RECKONING
Phil Ketchum

Five years of keeping himself alive in a brutal prison had made Brand tough and careless about who he gunned down . . .

FARGO: PANAMA GOLD
John Benteen

With foreign money behind him, Buckner was going to destroy the Panama Canal before it could be completed. Fargo's job was to stop Buckner.

FARGO:
THE SHARPSHOOTERS
John Benteen

The Canfield clan, thirty strong were raising hell in Texas. Fargo was tough enough to hold his own against the whole clan.

PISTOL LAW
Paul Evan Lehman

Lance Jones came back to Mustang for just one thing — revenge! Revenge on the people who had him thrown in jail.

HELL RIDERS
Steve Mensing

Wade Walker's kid brother, Duane, was locked up in the Silver City jail facing a rope at dawn. Wade was a ruthless outlaw, but he was smart, and he had vowed to have his brother out of jail before morning!

DESERT OF THE DAMNED
Nelson Nye

The law was after him for the murder of a marshal — a murder he didn't commit. Breen was after him for revenge — and Breen wouldn't stop at anything . . . blackmail, a frameup . . . or murder.

DAY OF THE COMANCHEROS
Steven C. Lawrence

Their very name struck terror into men's hearts — the Comancheros, a savage army of cutthroats who swept across Texas, leaving behind a bloodstained trail of robbery and murder.

SUNDANCE: SILENT ENEMY
John Benteen

A lone crazed Cheyenne was on a personal war path. They needed to pit one man against one crazed Indian. That man was Sundance.

LASSITER
Jack Slade

Lassiter wasn't the kind of man to listen to reason. Cross him once and he'll hold a grudge for years to come — if he let you live that long.

LAST STAGE TO GOMORRAH
Barry Cord

Jeff Carter, tough ex-riverboat gambler, now had himself a horse ranch that kept him free from gunfights and card games. Until Sturvesant of Wells Fargo showed up.

McALLISTER
ON THE
COMANCHE CROSSING
Matt Chisholm

The Comanche, McAllister owes them a life — and the trail is soaked with the blood of the men who had tried to outrun them before.

QUICK-TRIGGER COUNTRY
Clem Colt

Turkey Red hooked up with Curly Bill Graham's outlaw crew. But wholesale murder was out of Turk's line, so when range war flared he bucked the whole border gang alone . . .

CAMPAIGNING
Jim Miller

Ambushed on the Santa Fe trail, Sean Callahan is saved by two Indian strangers. But there'll be more lead and arrows flying before the band join Kit Carson against the Comanches.

GUNSLINGER'S RANGE
Jackson Cole

Three escaped convicts are out for revenge. They won't rest until they put a bullet through the head of the dirty snake who locked them behind bars.

RUSTLER'S TRAIL
Lee Floren

Jim Carlin knew he would have to stand up and fight because he had staked his claim right in the middle of Big Ike Outland's best grass.

THE TRUTH ABOUT SNAKE RIDGE
Marshall Grover

The troubleshooters came to San Cristobal to help the needy. For Larry and Stretch the turmoil began with a brawl and then an ambush.